BENEATH THE EARTH

LAURA GREENWOOD

SKYE MACKINNON

Peryton Press

To Gina, who fills our books with beauty.

The Seven Wardens series is a reverse harem, one woman and multiple love interests. Macey does not have to choose.

Please note that the authors of this book are from the UK, and as such, spellings and some turns of phrase will appear in British English.

You can find a glossary at the end of this book.

Once upon a time there was a kelpie Princess called Macey... or was there?

Having recently discovered she's not who she thought she was (Nessie might be her mother!), Macey has to put aside her personal life and focus on the Wardens' fight against the Mahoun and his cohorts.

At least now she has another ally in Rónán, a selkie who saved her from drowning after she defeated Self-Doubt, an evil creature that had been feeding off the Staran.

Most annoyingly of all, she hasn't been able to have any waffles yet. Maybe this time...

1. From the Deeps (Audiobook Available)
2. Into the Mists (Audiobook Available)
3. Beneath the Earth
4. Within the Flames
5. Above the Waves
6. Under the Ice
7. Rule the Dark

- Through the Storms (optional spin-off between books 1 & 2)
- Below the Baubles (optional short story between books 5 & 6)
- Beyond the Loch (optional novella set before the events of the Seven Wardens series)
- Inside the Egg (novella set after the events of the Seven Wardens series)

- Seven Wardens Boxed Set: Books 1-4
- Seven Wardens Boxed Set: Books 5-7
- Seven Wardens: The Complete Series

THE SEVEN WARDENS

Water: Macey (Kelpie)
Wind: Cam (Wraith)
Fire: Flint (Wraith)
Earth: Jared (Incubus)
Ice: Izban (Mage)
Lightning: Amber (Beithir)
Air: Talia (Seelie hosted within Macey)

ONE

A large, golden-brown waffle was floating towards Macey. Her mouth began to water as it came ever closer, its delicious scent steaming up her nose. This was heaven decorated with a honeycomb pattern. It was big enough to be breakfast, lunch and dinner, and maybe an afternoon snack as well.

She opened her mouth, ignoring the drool running down her chin -

"Macey, you're drooling all over me!"

"Maybe she's thinking of me?"

"Shut up, I want to sleep!"

The voices of her three men woke her. It was too early, and there were no waffles. She decided to go back to sleep. She'd not had enough rest for far too long and if her guys were going to shut up, she was going to sleep some more.

"Quiet," she muttered, her voice not quite functioning yet. And it didn't need to. Sleep was coming soon.

"What did you dream about?" Jared whispered. "Was it me?"

Macey growled groggily. Couldn't they just leave her alone?

"Waffles."

"Wait, she drooled because she was dreaming of waffles?" Flint said in mock outrage. "She's surrounded by the three of us and the memories of what we did last night, and she dreams of food?"

"Shut it," Macey yawned. "Let me sleep."

Jared snickered. "So you can dream of more waffles while the rest of us go hungry? No way. Come on, get up, let's find ourselves some breakfast."

Macey wanted to pull the blanket over her head, except that it turned out that Flint was being her blanket. His warm body was half draped over her, and his body heat was enough to keep her nice and cosy. As soon as he got up though, she was desperate for a proper duvet.

All three of her men left the bed and looked down at her naked body. She should have been embarrassed, but she actually enjoyed their slightly heated glances. If she wasn't so tired, she'd invite them to continue what they'd started the evening before. She smiled at the memory of being with all three of them. It had been a special moment, one that she would think of for years to come, that she was sure of. And hopefully, there'd be a lot more of these moments.

"I'll see if Amber and Izban are up yet," Cam excused himself and left her alone with the other two. They had one of the two bedrooms in the cottage, while the young couple had taken the other one.

When they'd returned to the house after their battle, the ghost had gone, hopefully he'd be reunited with Luch in the afterlife. Macey had been sad, but at the same time, she was happy for them. He'd waited for her for so long, he deserved to be with her for eternity. She'd asked her men if they believed in an afterlife, but they hadn't been able to give her a satisfying answer. Flint and Cam were so long-lived that they didn't care much about life after death. Jared's kind had legends about a land of roses and endless beaches where the dead were reunited with their loved ones. He didn't seem convinced, but that's just what Macey felt about the tales she'd grown up with. One deep ocean full of beauty and song. Waves that were strong and carried them onwards, to the next life.

"Are you going to get dressed?" Flint distracted her from her thoughts.

"That depends on what we're doing today," Macey

grumbled. "I don't want to fight, run or save anyone. My plan is to eat, sleep and cuddle."

Flint laughed. "I love how you included cuddling. I'm sure that can be arranged." He gave her a cheesy wink and she cringed.

"No cuddling if you look at me like that."

"Like what?" He put his hands on his hips in mock outrage.

"Like a dumb cartoon prince."

"Did you have cartoons in the water?"

Macey laughed. "No, but I caught up on my Earth entertainment education once I'd moved to the surface. My brothers had a TV and I had a lot of boring afternoons."

"I didn't take you for a couch potato."

She threw a pillow at him which he evaded effortlessly.

He grinned. "I guess pillow fights weren't part of your education?"

Macey growled and threw another one at him. Only one left; this pillow was going to have to count.

Flint turned the cushion he'd caught in his hands, as if trying to find the perfect grip to throw it.

Noticing that she was far too large a target, Macey sat up and pulled her legs close to her chest, hiding some of her nakedness.

"Yummy," Jared suddenly said, reminding Macey that her and Flint weren't alone in the room. The incubus was leaning against the wall, lazily watching them.

"What's yummy?" Macey asked in confusion.

"You. The sexual tension. It's an excellent breakfast."

"There is no sexual tension," Macey protested weakly, knowing that it was a lie. There was a lot of tension in the room. She could see the way Flint was looking at her. He was trying not to stare at her nakedness, but occasionally, his eyes flicked to her chest. She had to admit that she was quite enjoying his attention, but Jared using them as his breakfast... that was weird.

"Get out!" she told him, and with a smirk and a wave, the incubus left.

Macey huffed when she realised that she wasn't tired anymore. She was wide awake, actually, and now that she was sitting up, it really didn't make much sense to go back to sleep. Maybe Cam had managed to organise some proper breakfast. Food, human food, not the weird stuff Jared was consuming. Although he also ate proper food, so maybe he'd just been joking?

Her men were weird, but that was the way she liked them. Better weird than boring.

Without warning, she threw her remaining pillow at Flint and then jumped out of bed before he could retaliate. Her clothes lay discarded in a corner and with a disappointed sigh, she put them on. The house her men were living in was magical and cleaned her clothes overnight. This house... not so much. She couldn't wait to get back home. All this running and saving the world was getting exhausting. Not long ago, she'd been an innocent little loch kelpie and now, she'd been a prisoner, had fallen in love with three men and had seen death take one of her friends.

Life had become very complicated very quickly.

THE OTHERS WERE SAT around the long benches that they'd first encountered here. Izban had an arm around Amber, and the beithir was leaning into him, a satisfied sleepy grin on her face.

Macey knew that look. She was probably sporting it herself this morning. Maybe they could steal some girl time to talk about it. Maybe... she wasn't completely convinced by that. She'd never really had a close female friend before and didn't know what she was supposed to talk about with one.

Sex was a normal topic, right? As were men? It seemed like as good a starting point as any. But would Macey's antics scare the younger woman off? It wasn't like most people took three men to their bed at once. In fact, most didn't.

Macey straightened her spine. She loved her three

men. There was no denying that. And what she did with those three men, individually, or together, was her business, and hers alone. She'd talk about it if and when Amber asked, but not before. She didn't want to push her lifestyle on anyone else.

A short giggle escaped her. She had a lifestyle. She'd never expected that.

"Morning," Rónán said, not as brightly as the others.

A pang of guilt shot through Macey as she noticed his drawn features, and puffy eyes. He hadn't slept nearly as well as the rest of them. Maybe she should have offered him the room she'd shared with her men.

A firm hand rested on her back. "Don't even go there," Flint whispered in her ear.

Rónán's gaze shifted from what he was doing, and settled on Macey, raking her up and down as he did. She shifted from side to side, wondering if he could tell what she'd been up to. Or worse. If he'd heard the cries she was sure she made the night before.

She didn't even remember much of what her men had done to her specifically. Her main thought had been on the sensations they'd been giving her and the pleasure it brought.

Rónán's eyes met hers, and he winked.

He definitely knew what she'd been up to. Macey counted crabs in her head, trying not to think about it. If she didn't, then she could avoid the embarrassment that would bring.

"Morning," she muttered.

"Tea?" Rónán asked.

She nodded enthusiastically.

"There isn't much milk," he said apologetically.

"That's okay, I'll take it without." She gave him a weak smile.

Jared sucked in a shocked breath, the air whistling through his teeth. "Sacrilege," he whispered.

Macey shot him a withering look while Amber chuckled away.

"It's really not that bad," the beithir said. "We didn't always have milk up the mountain."

"That doesn't sound right," the incubus replied.

Rónán passed Macey a cup. Their fingers brushed and Macey could have sworn some kind of jolt of electricity passed between them. But that wasn't right. Amber was the electric one.

Glancing over her shoulder, Macey reassured herself that he hadn't noticed anything odd between her and Rónán. She wanted to be oblivious too, but the thought of what she'd felt was spinning around her head.

"What do we do now?" She didn't aim her question at anyone in particular, but instead hoped that someone would take her cue.

"Is there anything anyone needs?" Cam asked the room in response.

Most of them shook their heads, and murmured nos. But Macey actually stopped to consider. While she felt better rested than before, she didn't feel completely at peace with herself. Something was definitely up.

"Waffles?" she suggested with a cheeky grin. "Or home. I think I need a swim," she admitted hastily.

Jared gave her an appraising look, with a much more serious expression on his face than normal.

"Are you feeling okay?" he asked.

"Just a little worn," she replied. Maybe she should have worried about being so honest in front of people she barely knew. Rónán was still a complete mystery, and she hardly knew Izban beyond the fact he hadn't liked her at first. Technically, she barely knew Amber either, but somehow their imprisonment superseded that.

"Maybe Cam can try and make waffles again," Jared prompted.

"Try?" Amber asked, amusement glinting in her green eyes.

"Last time didn't go quite to plan," Jared replied, a little more jovial again.

"It was the waffle iron," Cam grumbled, not meeting anyone's eyes. "I'll try again for Macey though." He looked up, his grey swirling eyes meeting hers, and filled with so much love, it almost floored her.

How had she ended up here? Sure, the saving the world stuff was a little bit tiring. While being kept a prisoner of the Voice wasn't exactly enjoyable either, she'd gained so much more by leaving the Loch. She had her men, who were all more than willing to show her how much they loved her, and she had the beginnings of a best friend too. Something she'd never had before.

Despite the Voice trying to kill them all, and the Staran dying, she had a good life. Certainly better than most kelpies got.

She could definitely use a swim though. A swim and some tasty sweet pastries. Both of those would be good. Then maybe another night wrapped in her men's arms...

"Where would we go?" Amber asked Izban softly.

"Where ever you wanted to," he replied, his voice low and intimate.

"You'll come with us," Flint responded. "Our house grows as and when we need it to. And it's probably better we're all in the same place, just in case..." he trailed off.

"Basically for when the next thing goes wrong," Jared joked before taking a swig of his tea.

Macey grimaced, able to feel the heat of her own

through the mug she was holding. How he was letting that touch his throat was beyond her.

"Would you like to come too?" she asked Rónán, unsure what it was that was making her ask. It just felt right to. And if there was one thing she was certain of, it was her own gut feelings.

Most of the time anyway. Her gut feeling had led to her to nearly drown herself, so maybe she shouldn't put so much stock in it.

"Yes," he replied. "Though I will need to come back here."

"I think we all will," Cam muttered ominously.

TWO

The house was just like Macey remembered. Big, airy and cosy. She let the others show Amber, Izban and Rónán around and headed to the swimming pool. On the way, she begged the house to make the water pure, without chlorine. The guys had told her that the house fulfilled wishes and needs, so surely it wouldn't hurt asking?

The chemicals in the pool had made her skin itch last time, but she really needed a swim. Her kelpie form was threatening to burst out any moment. She'd not felt the urge this strongly in a long time. Usually it took at least a week without shifting for her to feel that way. She'd been swimming yesterday, back at St Kilda, so it didn't make any sense for her to be that desperate. Strange. Maybe her body was making up for all the shifts she wasn't able to do while in the

Voice's prison. Back there, she hadn't felt the urge, but there had also been no magic, so maybe that had stopped it.

When she reached the swimming pool, she breathed in deeply, then smiled. No chlorine. Just fresh, beautiful sea water.

"Thank you, house," she whispered, feeling a little silly about talking to the tiled walls around her.

She took off her clothes as fast as she could and jumped into the cool water, shifting almost as soon as she hit the surface. It was the fastest she'd ever shifted. One second, she was human, the next, a large, scaled kelpie.

She breathed in a large gulp of water and expelled it back through her gills. Oh, it was the most amazing feeling.

She whinnied loudly and began to swim back and forth, occasionally jumping out of the water to enjoy the splash of tiny droplets against her smooth scales.

This was her element. Her home.

With a happy swirl of her tail, she extended her magic, letting it soak up the water's energy. She felt as if she hadn't been in water for years. As if she'd been dying of thirst. It was strange, but she didn't care, as long as she was able to stay in the pool. Maybe the guys could bring her waffles. Things tasted different when she was in her kelpie form, but waffles surely had to be good no matter what, right?

A change in the energy around her made her resurface and look around the room. Rónán was standing by the edge of the pool, looking at her with a smile.

"Can I join you?"

Did that mean that he was going to change into a seal? Macey didn't know much about selkies, except that they took off their seal skins when they came onto land. But where was his skin? Or was that all just a legend and he was a regular shifter like her? Selkies were strange.

She whinnied in agreement and he began to take off his clothes. Pointedly, she turned around, not wanting to see his selkie bits. She had her own three men, thank you very much. As sexy as he was... no, she didn't just think that. He wasn't sexy. Well, he was, but not in that way. Weren't three men enough? There was only so much testosterone a kelpie could cope with.

A splash alerted her to his presence in the pool. Curiously, she turned, expecting a seal swimming in the water. But no, he wasn't a seal at all. He was just as human as he'd been moments before, except that he was now naked.

The disadvantage of being the only kelpie here was that nobody could understand her. She tried looking at him questioningly, but her eyes kept wandering beneath the surface, and that was plain rude.

"Why aren't you a seal?" she asked in her kelpie click language, but he just looked at her in confusion.

She whinnied in frustration. Maybe they should have this conversation later on, when she was human again.

"Can I touch you?" he suddenly asked, stunning her. What was he on about? That wasn't really a polite question to ask a lady. She wasn't a horse to be stroked. He'd never ask that if she'd been human...

She flicked her tail and swam away from him, hoping he'd get the message.

"Sorry, that was impolite!" he called. "It's just that it's supposed to be good luck to touch a kelpie, and I think we could all use a bit of good luck at the moment."

She'd never heard that before. If it was true, kelpies themselves had to be the luckiest creatures ever. Definitely just a legend, but obviously, Rónán believed in it. Or he was just using it as an excuse. Either way, Macey was intrigued. Flattered, almost.

Forgoing her pride, she approached him again. When she was in touching distance, she stopped, using her tail and webbed hooves to stay in position. Kelpies may not be the prettiest beings, but they were adapted perfectly to life underwater.

Rónán stretched out a hand and gently touched her muzzle. No human - or selkie - had ever touched her there before. And not in the gently, admiring way Rónán was. When kelpies met, they rubbed their cheeks together, but this was different. His hand was small on her forehead, running over her smooth scales.

"You're beautiful," he muttered. "Thank you."

With one final stroke, he retracted his hand, leaving her bereft of his touch. Maybe she should ask her men to do the same to her the next time she was swimming. She'd never realised how good human touch could feel.

"We should go back, Cam was busy burning the kitchen when I left," Rónán said with a wink. "I'll let you change in peace."

He climbed out of the water, showing Macey his perfectly formed arse. Despite her reservations, she was more and more tempted to add him to her men. One more couldn't hurt, right? Even if he wasn't a Warden.

She shook her head with a whiny, appalled at her own thoughts. She'd only met him yesterday. This was her hormones overreacting for some reason. She wasn't thinking rationally.

Once he'd left the room, Macey shifted back. She wasn't really ready to be human again, but the magic word had made her change her mind. Waffles...

As soon as she left the pool, she wanted to jump

back in. The urge was still there, not as strong as before she went for a swim, but still very noticeable. That had never happened before.

She shook off the water dripping from her hair, then put on the bathrobe hanging from a hook on the wall. The house was being very considerate once again.

THREE

Thick smoke filled the corridor outside the pool room.

Wait...smoke? That wasn't right, where could it be coming from? Short of Flint accidentally setting fire to himself, there wasn't anything Macey could think of to explain what was going on.

Shouts and exclamations came along with the smoke and she picked up her pace, anxious to check her men were okay. Maybe they were under attack? But no, that couldn't be right. The house wasn't exactly easy to find for anyone. It seemed unlikely they were being attacked here.

Even so, she didn't want to risk it, and almost sprinted down the corridor towards the scene of the commotion.

Thankfully, the house seemed to take her panic

into account, and shrunk the corridor so she could get there faster. Maybe she should think of a name for the place as a way of thanks.

Flames flared up from the side, almost singeing Cam's eyebrows. Macey watched in bemused amazement as Cam and Jared half-panicked and tried to put it out...badly.

But at least they were perfectly safe. Other than the small fire, anyway.

"Dare I ask?" she said, raising her eyebrows.

"He tried to make waffles."

Macey turned to face Flint, who had appeared beside her. "And you're not going to help?"

"I don't think adding more flames are the best idea," he pointed out. "Why aren't you putting the fire out?"

"And miss watching this?" She waved her hand at the two of them who were now hopping up and down and looking like they were in a cartoon.

A small giggle escaped from Macey. They really were too funny.

"That's not very responsible," Flint teased.

"It's only a little fire," she pointed out, the panic having subsided now that she'd seen the extent of the issue. "How did it even start?"

"I told you, Cam was trying to make waffles."

"How did he start a fire by making waffles?" Her

mouth watered even thinking about the tasty goodness.

"We have no idea. But anything that involves baking, he just fails at miserably. If Cam ever offers you chocolate cake he made himself, run. It's seriously bad."

"But he's such a good cook?" Macey's gaze flicked between Cam and Flint. She really wasn't sure what to make of this revelation.

"Everyone has their faults."

"But not being able to cook waffles?" She was genuinely shocked. She'd watched people making them in the street, they seemed pretty straight forward.

"Is it a deal breaker for you?" Flint joked.

"I don't know, it just might be." She tapped a finger to her chin mockingly.

Flint leaned in, his breath tickling her ear. "Enough that you want to replace him?"

She didn't know if he was teasing or not, so turned to face him. He studied her, and she got the answer she needed.

"None of you are replaceable," she whispered. "Not in a million years."

"Good to know." Flint tilted her chin gently and tipped her head back. He lowered his lips so they almost touched hers. "But just so you know, we wouldn't be completely opposed to an addition."

Before she had time to think about what he'd just said, he pressed his lips against hers and took her in a kiss filled with love and affection. There was no doubt this kiss came from someone who cherished her.

"Macey, will you stop snogging Flint and help?" Cam's slightly panicked tone broke through the moment.

"Oh no, keep kissing Flint, please," Jared countered. Cam shot him a dirty look, and Jared shrugged. "It's giving me a good top up."

Macey gave him a withering look. "Will you stop snacking on my sexual tension?"

"Not even if it was possible," Jared replied. "I was getting some off you earlier, too," he added, a knowing look in his eyes.

"What help do you want?" she asked Cam instead of responding to Jared's insinuation.

"Putting out the fire," he pointed out.

She grimaced, feeling a little guilty about not thinking that one through. Of course he wanted her to put out the fire, she was the one who could do it easily.

Summoning her magic from within, she created a small ball of water in her hands, before sending it towards the flames with a gentle push.

Except, there was nothing gentle about what happened then. The ball spun a couple of times, growing in size as it hurtled towards the flames and Cam. Macey desperately tried to pull the water back to her, but nothing she tried seemed to actually be working.

Instead, she watched in horror as the ball reached the fire, drenching the entire kitchen, along with Cam and the flames. Next to her, Flint began to laugh uncontrollably.

"I'm sorry," she squeaked.

"At least it put out the flames," Jared said, struggling to hold back the laughter himself.

"Why does the kitchen look like a monsoon just tore through it?" Rónán asked, making Macey cringe. She hadn't intended for him to find out about her little accident, though how she'd thought to keep it a secret with her men around was a mystery.

"Thanks, I think?" Cam held his sopping wet arms away from his body, his clothes dragging downwards with the weight of the water. "I'm going to go dry off," he added.

"What happened?" Rónán said softly.

"I lost control." She looked down at the floor, and scuffed it with her bare foot. "Apparently," she added reluctantly.

"Has this happened before?" he asked.

Macey shook her head. "I had decent control before my dad locked my powers. But I've only just got them back..." She did have to wonder if it was something to do with the previous block.

"Hmm." Rónán appeared lost in thought, and the last thing she wanted to do was disturb him. She barely knew the man, she didn't want to anger him unnecessarily. "I might be able to help," he said eventually.

"You can?" Her eyes lit up at the prospect.

"Yes, if you're okay with that?" His earnest expression letting on just how serious he was.

"It is with me..." She looked around her own men, before resting her gaze on Flint, who was standing closest.

He shrugged. "It's not our choice, Macey. If this is something you want, then we're okay with it."

Somehow, that sounded like Flint was talking about more than just some magic practice with Rónán. Macey shook her head. No, that was not something she was going to think about. Three men were enough, right? A girl could only deal with so much testosterone... and lack of waffles. Could Rónán bake?

"I think we should be near water for this," the selkie suggested.

"But we just left the swimming pool," Macey protested. "I want some food first."

She ignored the feeling inside of her that told her to run to the pool and shift again. That feeling wasn't supposed to be there, so maybe if she didn't pay it any attention, it would go away.

"I'd cook something, but the stove..." Cam pointed to the smoking remains of the cooker.

"Can't the house provide us with a takeaway or something?" Macey asked. Her stomach was growling; these men better give her some food.

Jared chuckled. "That's not how it works. But I'm sure Cam can whip up some sandwiches, he doesn't need the hob for that."

Cam nodded, already on the way to the fridge which had been spared from the flames. It was quite wet, though.

There was something wrong with her magic and Macey was determined to find out what, even if she had to ask a selkie for help. Oh, who was she kidding? She wanted his help, his company and his friendship. She'd not known him for long but it felt otherwise. Almost like it did with her three men.

Maybe it was just her hormones overacting. Kelpies only had their period every three months, but when it came, it was a lot stronger. It made her act like a horny teenager – much to the amusement of her brothers.

A pang of guilt tore at her heart. Her brothers were still in the Voice's dungeons and right now, she couldn't see any way of getting them out of there. At least they now had a better idea of what the Voice was. That had to be an advantage.

"Egg and cress or cheese and onion?" Cam asked and she forced herself to focus on the present. And on the food.

"Both?"

He smirked and got to work. She loved how he made hers first, the vegetarian sandwiches, while the others had to wait for their dead animal version.

Although she did pity them a little when she took her first bite and they all stared at her with hungry expressions.

Sorry, boys.

SHE SHIFTED ALMOST AS SOON as her body hit the water. Rónán wanted to have their lesson outside of the swimming pool, but Macey ignored him, the pull of the water too much to resist. Her human mind told her that it was wrong, that she usually had more control, but the kelpie side whinnied happily and dived to the bottom of the pool. Macey missed the loch she'd grown up in, its various shades of green, the kelp at the bottom that would gently tickle her scales when she swam through it, the delicate warmth of the sun rays breaking through the surface.

Maybe they could put in a little stopover at the loch. Her father may not even know that her brothers were imprisoned... although no, Nessie would have told them.

Nessie.

Macey growled at the thought of her aunt who might be more than just that. The kelpie she'd trusted and who may have lied to her entire life. She refused to think of the m-word in relation to her. Macey already had parents and they were her parents, no matter what she'd been told. Her father was the kelpie king and her mother his wife.

Oops, she thought the m-word.

"Macey!" Rónán called out loud enough for her to hear below the surface. Macey turned and saw he was sitting on the edge of the pool, his legs dangling in the water. With a grin, she swam towards him and gently rubbed her head against the soles of his feet.

He laughed and wiggled his toes, giving her the most amazing head massage. The antenna on her forehead waved from side to side as if it wanted to touch his legs.

"You need to be human for our lesson," he said loudly, but she refused to resurface. She was a kelpie and she was going to enjoy the water for a bit longer. The solid ground could wait.

Macey playfully nipped at his leg and he cried out in surprise. Why didn't he want to play with her?

She gripped his other leg with her teeth and

pulled him into the water. With a splash, he entered the pool, her home. She wasn't going to leave this place. Why would she ever leave the water?

Her men could move in with her. Maybe the house was going to extend the swimming pool to make it big enough for all of them.

"Macey, stop it," Rónán spluttered, resurfacing.

Such a party pooper. She was just playing, why didn't he want to play with her? Maybe he liked it rough?

She dived lower and pulled on his legs again, making him stay below the surface. Why didn't he shift and join her? He was so boring as a human. They couldn't breathe for long in the water, she remembered that much even in the haze that her mind was trapped in.

Maybe if she kept him beneath the surface he'd shift. Maybe he needed some help with it. Just like young kelpies had trouble shifting into their human form and needed some encouragement.

Somehow, he slipped from her grip and swam up before she could stop him. As soon as his head resurfaced, he shouted, "I can't shift! Stop it, Macey! I can't shift!"

See, she'd known. He needed help with his shifting.

He was swimming fast to the edge of the pool, where the ladder was that made it easier to get out. Was he playing with me? Finally. She decided to give him a little head start. With his puny human legs, he wasn't very fast. He moved them differently from other humans though, as if they were sewn together at the thighs.

"What's going on?"

"Empty the pool!"

Who was speaking? She took a deep breath and lifted her head from the water to take a look. Jared was standing in the doorway, looking very confused.

Someone else to play with! She whinnied in delight.

"Empty the fucking pool!" Rónán shouted again. "She needs to get out of the water."

Jared stared at them for another moment, then ran to the wall to his right and pressed a button on the pad that controlled the water temperature.

A vibration went through the pool and a gurgling sound made her dive again. In all four corners, holes had begun to open and water was running into them, leaving the pool.

No!

She swam to the closest one and put one of her webbed hooves on top of it, stopping the water flow. But there were three more. She could feel the water disappearing, and with it, all the energy that sustained her.

It was happening fast. She needed to think. There

had to be a solution. She needed more water, but she couldn't do that kind of magic in her kelpie form. She needed to shift, and then she could summon more water, and fill the pool again.

She took in another deep breath, making oxygen run through her gills, then started to shift.

It hadn't been this painful in a long time. Agony tore through her as her hooves formed into fingers and toes, her spine straightened and her scales turned back into smooth skin.

Macey screamed, water threatening to fill her lungs.

Suddenly, cool air surrounded her. Was she out of the water? No, even through her tear-filled eyes she could see that she was still at the bottom of the pool... but a large air bubble was forming around her. She spat out the water clogging up her throat and breathed in the fresh air.

What the waves was happening?

The air bubble began to move, taking her with it. She was drifting up, as if she was flying, leaving the half-empty pool behind.

She was set down on the edge of the pool and immediately, four large men surrounded her, blocking her view of the water.

"Explain," Jared demanded, his incubus sultriness begging her to tell him everything. Except, she didn't know what to say. "I..." she trailed off, not knowing where to even start.

Flint crouched down next to her and slipped an arm around her shoulders, pulling her close as she shivered.

"It's okay," he whispered. "You can tell us."

"I don't know," Macey muttered, sniffing as tears began to well up in her eyes.

"I think I do," Rónán broke the silence which was already forming around them. Probably caused by none of the men quite knowing what to do with a broken kelpie.

"Tell me?" Macey whimpered.

Rónán sighed, before sitting down on the side of the pool, dangling his legs over the side and swinging them back and forth.

"She was doing what she was meant to," he said after a few more moments of quiet.

"I'm not meant to hurt anyone," Macey protested.

"No, maybe not you specifically. But kelpies. Your kind's reputation had to come from somewhere," he pointed out. "This is where. At least, I think so."

"That doesn't explain anything," Jared growled.

"It does," Rónán responded. "How long did she spend out of the water before St. Kilda?"

The men exchanged uneasy looks.

"We're not sure," Cam offered. "We lost track of time while she was trapped in the Voice's keep."

"It was two months, three weeks and four days." Amber's voice came from the doorway and Macey looked up to find the redhead leaning against there wood, with Izban just a couple of steps behind.

"You were counting?" Macey asked.

"Yes. I'm a beithir, we're connected to the weather. We have an odd way of being able to tell how much time has passed. I was in there for a month and two days before you arrived. It's not difficult to work out how long you'd been in there." Amber shrugged.

"You're amazing," Izban whispered, only to be ignored by the rest of them.

"But I did shift after that," Macey protested, though it sounded weak even to her own ears. "I was in the cseag's pool and then again on St. Kilda..."

"Yes, but not for any substantial amount of time," Rónán countered. "You need to regularly spend time in the water, if you don't, then this will happen. And the longer you go without, the longer you need to be underneath to recharge."

"And not doing that will turn me into a homicidal maniac?"

"Technically, I'm not human, so it'd be a selikicidal maniac."

"Helpful," she muttered.

"That is the other thing..." he trailed off, seeming reluctant to continue.

"Yes?"

"There are two ways to recharge yourself. The first is being underwater for a prolonged period of time. The other is to, erm...how to put this...devour men."

"Devour as in eat, or devour as in..."

"With an incubus as one of your companions, I doubt you have any problems in the latter department," Rónán pointed out.

"Oh."

"It doesn't matter," Flint reassured her.

"Not at all," Jared added.

Anger bubbled up within Macey and she shrugged off Flint's arm, jumping to her feet. "It's hardly fine. By the waves, what's wrong with you?!" she shouted.

Jared opened his mouth to speak but Macey held her hand up, stopping him in his tracks.

"Don't you dare tell me it's okay. This is far from okay. What if next time it's Flint I pull under water? What then?" A sob strangled her as she finished speaking, the emotions of the moment overwhelming her.

"Then we'll just make sure Flint stays away from the water," Cam suggested, his voice a lot calmer than the others.

"And how long is that solution actually going to work for? He can't avoid water around me forever?" Her voice cracked as she spoke, but none of them moved to comfort her. They probably figured it would be wasted at the moment. With her emotions all over the place, there was a good chance she'd end up refilling the water and pushing them in.

Angry tears rolled down her cheeks, her whole body vibrating with power.

A wave of something undefined rose within her and she was dimly aware of people shouting. Macey was fairly sure all but one person had left the room, but she couldn't be certain, there was something too confusing about the situation.

"Macey, I need you to listen to me," the man still in the room said. She still couldn't tell which one of them it was but she was grateful for his presence.

Or fearful of it. If he was here, then he was in danger from whatever was growing inside her.

It wasn't unlike a shift. Except that it also wasn't. She didn't need to change forms, this was bigger than that.

"Macey, I need you to let go."

She shook her head, not sure how to even start following his instructions. She almost doubted they'd work at all.

"I know it's hard, but you need to. If you don't..." he trailed off, his own voice shaking a little. "If you don't, then you'll likely end up imploding inwards and none of us really want to deal with that."

"I can't," she sobbed. "I can't, I can't, I can't." She

kept repeating the word as the thing inside her built up more, threatening to burst free. She couldn't let it though. Not with someone else's life at risk.

"You can," the voice said in a sing song way. "Just listen to me."

A strange humming filled the air. She found the lyric sounds rather soothing and relaxed a little more, thought the threat of an explosion still lingered.

The sensation increased more and she knew she wouldn't be able to hold it back much longer, there was too much inside her. Too much she couldn't contain.

Opening her mouth, Macey began to scream. The sound wrenched through the air along with the pitter patter of rain and a whooshing sensation she'd only ever associated with the wind.

More power filled her than she'd ever experienced in her life before. If she wasn't so scared of it, she'd laugh at the thrill of it.

After what seemed like an age, and yet no time later, the feeling suddenly stopped and Macey collapsed to the floor in a heap, no longer able to keep her eyes open.

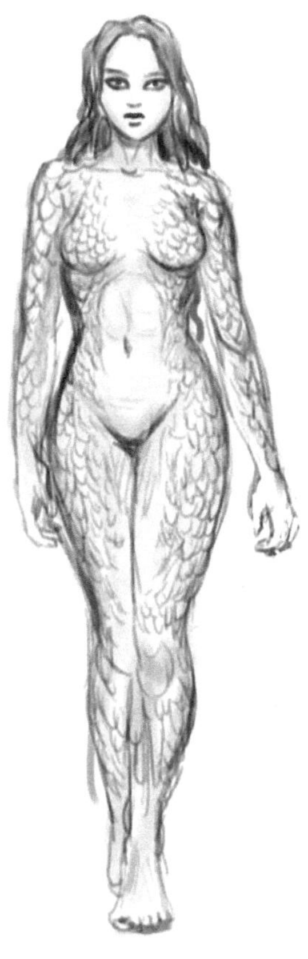

Macey

FOUR

Little selkie, little seal,
In the morning you will feel
Brush of waves in sea so deep
I will hold you while you sleep.

Macey woke to the same voice that had sung to her just before she'd fallen unconscious. This time, however, she recognised who it was. Rónán.

The selkie's baritone was rich and warm, embracing her, making her feel like he was hugging her.

Which was also true. She was lying on his lap, his arms around her chest, holding her while singing his lullaby. It felt rather good to be in his arms. She resisted smiling, not wanting him to know that she was awake.

"Little selkie, little seal,
Careful now, or they will steal
Keep your one true skin all wrapped
or you'll be forever trapped."

The tune turned sadder, and Macey couldn't help but ask, "Is that what happened to you?"

"You're awake," Rónán said, stating the obvious. "How are you feeling?"

Macey took a quick inventory of her body. There wasn't any pain, but she did feel a strange tingling in her limbs.

"Fine, I think. What exactly happened?"

"Do you want the long or the short version."

"Short," she replied impatiently.

"You glowed. All the pipes burst. The pool refilled itself. It started raining inside the house. And... ehm... you've got scales."

"What?!"

Macey shot up from her comfortable position on Rónán's lap and looked at her arms. They were covered in tiny, smooth scales, just like the ones she had when she was in her kelpie form. Except that right now, she was human. Her bare legs were the same, the scales reflecting the light of the brightly lit pool room.

"By the fucking waves," she muttered, inspecting her hands and feet. There was no webbing, luckily, and the scales were smaller and lighter, blending in a little more but still distinctly non-human.

"My face?" she asked, turning to Rónán.

"No scales," he said and she sighed in relief. That's when she noticed that Rónán was bare chested, his chiseled abs capturing her gaze.

"What happened to your shirt?"

She knew she was distracting both herself and him, but he seemed happy to oblige.

He grinned. "You're wearing it. I thought you'd be more comfortable waking up with some clothes rather than being naked."

"Thanks, I guess." She really didn't want to think about the fact that he'd dressed her. That she'd probably been in his lap, naked. That he was shirtless. That she was almost drooling.

She turned away from him, chastising herself for wanting the selkie. She already had three men. That was two more than most women had. How could she be this greedy? And why was she thinking about Rónán when she had suddenly turned into a scaled monster?

She shook off the thoughts of devouring Rónán... wait. The guys had used that word. No, it had been Rónán. He'd been talking about her devouring men. Was that what was happening to her? Was she turning into a wanton kelpie, feeding off sex like incubi?

Even now, she was fighting against the urge to turn and kiss Rónán. Was this what Jared felt? If so, she was gaining a new sense of admiration for him. He was so in control most of the time, not jumping her like she was wanting to jump Rónán. Maybe she should get away from the selkie and spend some time with her men instead. But they weren't here and Rónán was.

"Slap me," she whispered.

"What?"

"I want things I shouldn't. Slap me out of it."

Rónán chuckled. "I'm not going to hit you."

"Then get away from me."

She wanted to scramble off his lap, run away from him, but she couldn't make herself do it.

Why wasn't she freaking out about the scales? Why was she so... horny instead?

"Something's happening to me," she said quietly. "I feel things I shouldn't be feeling. Where are the guys? I need them here, not you."

She didn't turn around to see if he looked hurt by her words.

"It's too dangerous for Flint just now, his fire would be too vulnerable to all the water magic you have filling the the air just now. Jared would love to be here, but... ehm... his incubus got a little out of hand when he felt your pull. Cam is busy holding him back or you'd have an incubus screwing you mindless just now. And you know incubi can kill when they get out of control, right?"

She nodded, stunned.

"Which leaves me. I might be the one least likely to get hurt if your magic overwhelms you again." His voice was more serious now, containing none of the previous humour.

"But why is this happening?" Macey asked. "All this just because I didn't shift for a long time? I've never heard of this happening to other kelpies, and I know a few who've been living on land for ages."

Rónán was quiet for a moment, then said, "I think it's a combination of things. First, not shifting for months. Then, being under the influence of the creature you call the Voice. Third, you had some weird shit happen to you when you fought the creature hurting the Staran. And additionally, the Staran failing has started having an effect on all magic, not just yours. One of these might not be enough to have that much of an effect, but all four together..."

"Turned me into a monster," Macey finished his sentence.

Suddenly, he grabbed her by the shoulders and turned her around. "You're not a monster. You're a beautiful, strong, magnificent woman. Don't you ever call yourself a monster again."

Macey raised her arms, showing him her scales. "Look at me! I'm deformed. I'm a -"

His lips shut her up.

His kiss was different from the others, but no less enticing. Macey pushed up against him, the memory of her new scales already sinking backwards. What did it matter if she had them when a hot selkie was making his feelings known to her?

Her whole body heated up as she shifted against him and felt how hard he was against her. There were two ways she could go with this. Either she put a stop to it, or she went all the way. The former seemed to be a bit of a let down though. And her men had already given her the go ahead...

She twisted around, removing herself from his lap briefly so she could straddle him and link her legs around his back.

His hard cock pressed against her, heating her further as she rocked back and forth. The only issue being the clothing between the two of them. It was definitely in the way and she almost wished she had magic that would vanish the little they were wearing.

Rónán's hand slipped beneath his shirt, caressing the skin of Macey's back. She shivered in anticipation.

"Are you sure about this?" he whispered against her lips. "I don't want you to-"

"Stop talking and kiss me." She pressed her lips against his with more vigour, pulling him closer with her arms around his neck.

Rónán cupped her ass and moved her so she was laying down against the side of the pool, the rough, cold floor a welcome sensation.

Macey moaned as he thrust against her.

"Off," she murmured. "I need you."

Rónán broke away from her and shimmied slightly so he could remove his jeans. Macey propped herself up and whipped off the shirt which was covering her, leaving them both gloriously naked.

He lowered himself over her, their skin slick where it touched. Leaning down, Rónán captured her lips in a deep kiss which she felt throughout her body. Macey arched back into him, desperate to feel more of him. To have him inside her and feel complete.

Something told her this wasn't going to be like with her other men. This wasn't contrasting elements coming together. This was two water beings becoming one for the first time. She didn't even care that he was a selkie. Not if he made her feel like this.

"Please," she begged, slipping her hand between them as Rónán rocked against her.

He trailed kisses down her neck and grabbed her hand, stopping it from wondering further. "Not yet." His deep voice rumbled against her skin, only serving to excite her further.

Rónán's lips continued to travel downwards, one of his hands moving up the outside of Macey's thigh. Her legs fell open of their own accord, inviting him in. Rónán chuckled before taking one of her nipples into his mouth and flicking it with his tongue.

Macey arched into him, a soft gasp escaping from her. Rónán took the sound as encouragement and repeated the movement.

She gasped again, secretly wanting to demand more but scared to. If she interrupted him, then maybe he'd stop.

He switched to her other breast, suckling on her other nipple as he drew his hand inwards, hovering it not quite close enough to her centre and where she wanted him most.

"Did you know selkies can hold their breath for a really long time?" Rónán asked as he kissed down her stomach.

She shook her head, almost unable to think though the sensations throughout her body.

"Would you like me to show you?" He blew gently across the skin of her hip, causing her to buck slightly. If this was how she was acting when he wasn't even touching her properly, how was it going to be when he finally filled her?

Somehow, she managed to nod, accompanying it with a slight moan.

Rónán propped himself up and watched intently as he slipped his finger inside her. Macey's mind went blank, unable to form any kind of rational thought.

He lowered his head, kissing up the inside of her

thighs as she squirmed against him. Without waiting any longer, he settled between her legs, drawing his tongue upwards, tasting her thoroughly.

If she hadn't been able to think before, then this was something entirely new. He hooked his fingers inside her, pressing on just the right spot to make her insides begin to coil tighter.

Macey lost track of time, the feeling inside her getting more and more intense with every movement of Rónán's fingers and tongue. Small gasps and moans fell from her lips and she wasn't truly in control of what her body was doing.

As suddenly as he'd started, Rónán pulled away, climbing back up her body and taking her in a searing kiss that left little doubt about what he was going to do next.

She felt his hand cover his cock and guide it towards her. Then with one firm thrust, he seated himself inside her. The full feeling was more than welcome, and while her body was coiling itself up tighter, something else deep within relaxed. She hadn't even been aware she was so on edge.

Well, that was a lie. She'd been well aware there was something angry inside her. She'd been able to feel it before she and Rónán had started this.

They fell into a rhythm that only they knew. Rónán's pants mingled with hers and all that surrounded them was the sounds of sex.

Inside her, the feeling grew impossible to contain and the second Rónán's thrusts increased in speed, she let go. A drawn-out moan filled the air as her body exploded, the wave of passion crashing through her and refreshing her in a way she was both familiar with and was also completely new.

Moments later, Rónán followed her over the edge, groaning his own release into her ear, only increasing her own pleasure.

He withdrew from her, dropping a kiss on her forehead and collapsing down next to her. Rónán pulled her closely and Macey made contented noises as she snuggled into him. His presence was calming after the intensity of their previous activities. Knowing that he was close, she closed her eyes and let herself drift off to exhausted, peaceful sleep.

FIVE

Everyone was sitting around the kitchen table when Rónán and Macey returned, even Amber and Izban. He had an arm around her shoulders and she was snuggled against his chest. Macey had to stop herself from making a cooing sound at the sight of their cuteness. Did she have that same adoring look in her eyes when she looked at her men?

Apropos, her men. Jared, Cam and Flint were all looking at her with barely veiled curiosity. There was no jealousy or irritation in their expressions at all, simply the desire to know what happened. Or was the curiosity because of her new scales? Wait a moment, the scales had disappeared. She looked at her arms and legs. No scales. She was human again, at least on the outside. Had it all been a one-off or was she going to turn scaly again soon?

Macey sat down besides Flint and waited for Rónán to take a seat on her other side, before she cleaned her throat.

"Rónán helped me deal with my magic," she began. "Sorry for bursting your pipes."

Cam laughed loudly. "You can burst my pipes anytime, little kelpie."

"Mine too," Jared grinned. "Although please give us some warning next time so we can ask the house for more buckets and mops. Or a pump."

"That bad?" Macey asked, feeling more guilty by the second.

Flint reached over and put an arm around her shoulders, squeezing reassuringly. "Nothing we couldn't handle. We've had parties here that were more destructive than your magic, so don't worry. Are you feeling better?"

Macey nodded. "Yes, I think I've got it all back under control." She blushed a little. "Rónán helped."

She was kind of expecting a reaction from her guys, but none came. Sure, they had insinuated that they were fine with her adding someone to her harem, but that didn't mean they'd not feel jealousy.

Amber chuckled in amusement and all eyes turned to the beithir. "I think your men were quite turned on by the idea that you were with the selkie," she said with a giggle.

"I wasn't," Cam protested at the same time as Jared admitted, "I was."

They looked at each other before Jared added, "But I'm an incubus. I can feel sexual energy from miles away."

"Cowards," Amber muttered, giving Macey a wide grin. "Are you planning on adding any more, Macey? I'm beginning to wonder what you're going to do with all of them. You'll need a larger bed."

Izban groaned and put a hand over his girlfriend's mouth. "Don't upset our hosts," he whispered loud enough for everyone to hear. He clearly wasn't as comfortable around the other Wardens as Amber was. Was he still suspicious of them all? Was he still intending to leave?

Cam cleared his throat. "Anyway, we should discuss our next steps. Just because we defeated the creature inhabiting the Staran doesn't mean that we can relax. There's more like it out there, including the Voice. He impersonates the Mahoun, the devil, and the one we killed was Self-Doubt. What other personas could these creatures have taken on? Fear? Anger? Loneliness?"

"This is an impossible task," Izban sighed. We don't even know who the enemies are, nor how to destroy them. Now that the Staran is mostly back to normal, maybe we should just be content with that and wait for the next generation of Wardens to take on the task."

Amber elbowed him in the ribs. "Don't."

"What?" He looked at her almost confused.

"Don't be an arsehole."

He frowned. "I'm not risking you for some fool-hardy venture that might get you killed."

Amber shut him up by kissing him on the lips, before turning to the rest of the group.

"Please continue, Cam," she said with a sweet smile. "Izban will listen now."

The blue-haired mage in question didn't look very happy about it, but said nothing further.

Cam hesitated for a moment as if waiting for Izban to protest, but then said, "I propose we go after the Voice first. We know that he exists, at least, and we now know what he is."

"Kind of," Jared interjected.

Cam sighed. "Kind of. we managed to destroy Self-Doubt, which fills me with hope that we might be able to deal with the Mahoun as well."

"In the prophecy, it says that Air will appear 'when the end is near'," Macey said deep in thought. "We now have Air. Does that mean this is only the calm before the storm? Is everything about to go pear shaped?"

Flint pulled her closer to him. "Even if the apocalypse is about to happen, we'll be together. We'll get through this."

Izban laughed mirthlessly. "There won't be an apocalypse. Don't make this sound worse than it is."

"You didn't see what I saw," Amber said quietly, pulling everyone's attention to her. "The Mahoun showed me things, terrible things. I think he wanted to weaken me by showing me how resistance was futile, how he was going to destroy the world. Back then, I didn't care much, I was too focussed on staying alive, but now that I've been away from him for a while, the images are coming back to me." She shuddered and her eyes darkened. "He's planning to do something to the ground, to the earth. I saw crops dying, cattle starving. He's not going to attack magic users this time. He's targeting humans."

"Not just humans," Jared said thoughtfully. "If the earth is sick, animals die. First the land animals, then the birds, the fish. Everything is connected and if the balance is disturbed, everyone is at risk. We may not realise it, but we're dependent on the humans and their resources." He got up, his fists clenched. "I need to go to Earth, check what's happening. If he's already started, I may be able to feel it, but not from here. We're too far removed from the human plane."

Cam turned to Amber, taking on the rule as the leader once more. "Do you know why the Mahoun is doing this? What is he trying to achieve?"

"I've asked myself that for a long time," she answered, her voice a little shakily. "But now I think he has no choice but to do evil. He took on the persona of the devil, and everyone expects the devil to cause death and destruction. The Voice, whatever creature he may be, is now fulfilling that role, finding ways to kill. Maybe he feeds on death like Self-Doubt did of the people travelling on the Staran. The problem is, people also think that the devil is immortal and invincible. I'm wondering if that might make it true."

"Nobody is invincible," Macey said more confidently than she felt. "We've defeated Self-Doubt itself, so we'll deal with the Voice just the same."

"Luch died for us to kill the Staran creature," Izban reminded her. "Who needs to die this time?"

"We'll find a way. Nobody is going to die. We're all coming out of this alive."

Rónán suddenly leant forwards. Macey had almost forgotten that the selkie was sitting next to her; he'd been unusually quiet.

"There's a selkie legend about the devil. We don't call him the Mahoun, but I assume it's the same one. In the stories, there is a way to kill him."

"How?" Macey asked, holding her breath in anticipation.

Indecision warred over Rónán's face, as if he didn't want to tell them at all. Hurt swelled within

Macey. After what they'd shared, she'd have thought he'd trust her more. Apparently not. She should have known better than to trust a selkie...

"It's how to explain it, Macey," Rónán interrupted her inward berating. "Not that I don't trust you with the information."

She scowled. "Right."

Rónán sighed.

"Let him speak," Flint said, leaning over to run a soothing hand over her back. She calmed her breathing, appreciating the support.

"Some of it is pure fiction. Like the idea that the devil is a giant orca..."

"An orca? Really?" Jared scoffed.

"I said that bit was pure fiction," Rónán reminded him, staying surprisingly calm given the accusation. "What seems more likely is that the devil takes on a different form depending on what you fear the most."

"Surely having your skin stolen would be the number one selkie fear?" Cam asked, curiosity tinging every word.

"Being eaten comes a close second," Rónán deadpanned.

"Not if Macey's doing the eating." Jared gave her a playful wink.

Macey stifled a giggle and forced a serious look back onto her face. Rónán hadn't missed the gesture though and smiled at her with a knowing glint in his eye.

"Later," he mouthed.

Heat flooded through her at the thought and she became flustered.

"The story," Izban prompted, his voice betraying how annoyed he was by the flirting.

Rónán cleared his throat. "Sorry, yes. So for me the devil would take the form of an orca, for Flint, perhaps a being made of water..."

"You realise our girlfriend is a water being?"

"Believe it or not, I had noticed," Rónán answered. "But she's not made of water. The devil will become whatever it has to in order to defeat you. There's even a rumour it can turn what you are against you. Whether that's burning a flame, breaking up the earth..."

"Or drowning in the water," Macey added softly. She tried not to think about her own experience drowning. To say it was unpleasant was an understatement.

"Exactly. It's a dangerous foe."

"Which is all well and good, but none of that gives us a way to actually defeat it," Jared pointed out, leaning back in his chair and seeming far too relaxed for the conversation. That was just him though. Macey knew him well enough by now to know he was just a chilled out person.

"By mastering more than one element."

Stunned silence greeted Rónán's revelation as it sank into the Wardens.

"You mean like Macey and Air?" Amber asked after a moment.

"No. Though I suspect that may help," Rónán replied. "More like what you did in the cave. You combined your powers."

"So why can't we just do that again?" Flint asked, cocking his head to the side in an adorably sexy way. Despite the fact she'd only been with Rónán a short time ago, Macey found her mind drifting towards what she could be doing with her other men...

"I don't think that's what Rónán is saying," Cam said, speaking for the first time since they'd arrived back with the others. "I think he's saying each of us needs to be able to control the other six elements."

"Pretty much," he acknowledged.

"How are we supposed to do that?" A forlorn feeling filled Macey. She wouldn't even know where to start controlling lightning like Amber, and she'd channelled the other woman's powers before. She had no chance with the rest of them.

"I'm not sure," Rónán admitted. "It's all just a folk tale. But after meeting the Wardens, it's difficult not to believe in them anymore. I've seen more than enough proof that your legend is real."

Each of them nodded in turn, except for Izban who sat there glaring.

"Why should we learn?" he demanded. "Put ourselves in danger to defeat something that may or may not exist?"

"Izban!" Amber scolded.

"He does have a valid question," Macey said, trying her best to keep her tone unassuming and them all out of the zone of anger. "But I do have a question for you."

The Ice Warden met her gaze. There was as little warmth as his title suggested in his eyes but Macey wasn't about to let that stop her. He would become a part of the team, or she'd do her best to replace him. The main thing stopping her working on that right away was that it would make her friend sad.

"Mahoun hurt Amber. Are you really going to let him just get on with whatever he's doing after that?"

The two Wardens stared off at each other, neither of them saying a word. The tension in the air grew thicker by the moment and Macey wanted to break it more than anything. But she knew if she did that there was a chance they'd lose Izban and she didn't know whether Amber would follow him or not. She hoped not, her friend had a good sense of right and wrong. But then again, she also loved Izban. If it was Macey in her place then she'd side with her men on anything. Even if they were being stubborn assholes.

"You win," Izban muttered eventually, tearing his eyes away.

Relief surged through Macey. For now, he was on her side. Though she wasn't sure if that'd always be the case. Hopefully they wouldn't need a moment like this again.

"Thank you," Amber mouthed at her.

Macey gave the other woman a weak smile. At least she knew where the beithir's loyalties lay. She wanted to stand by the Wardens.

"Right, so back to square one. How do we learn to control all of the elements?" Macey asked the assembly.

"I'm not sure," Rónán answered. "That's as much as I know about the legend. It specified controlling each of the seven elements and that was the key to defeating the devil, nothing more than that."

"Wait, just one person controlling all the elements?" Cam specified.

"I guess." Rónán shrugged. "But why one and not seven?"

"Because there's only one person here with tattoos of all seven elements," Cam replied.

Six sets of eyes turned to Macey and she gulped.

By the waves, she was in trouble.

Malan, the Prophet

SIX

Making plans had been easy. Putting them into practice, not so much. Just because Macey had the markings didn't mean that she knew how to use them. For all she knew, she needed a spell or magic word to activate them.

It was Jared's idea to seek out Malan again. So far, the prophet had been quite helpful, mostly, so chances were that he had some advice for them now. Which meant that they were on the road again - well, the Staran. Izban and Amber stayed back at the house to look through the library, hoping to find something about the markings. It was probably a waste of time, but Macey was quite glad to be alone with her men again. It was like back when they'd started their strange journey. Except that now, they also had Rónán with them.

"Do you think he'll have waffles this time?" Jared whispered to her as they stepped into the mists, and Macey laughed out loud, drawing the looks of the other guys.

"Waffles," she explained, and they all nodded sagely. It had become more than just a running joke. It was something binding them all together. How romantic, the search for waffles. Maybe getting them would be a disappointment, an anticlimax. Sometimes the quest was more exciting than the treasure, after all.

Travelling the Staran felt strange this time, like they were calmer somehow. Maybe that was how it was supposed to feel, not as stomach-upsetting as it had been in the past while Self-Doubt was still eating away at them.

As soon as they stepped out of the mist, Malan's bodiless head was staring at them. He hovered over a bench outside his little cottage, as if he was sitting on it. It looked ridiculous, but Macey knew better than to laugh. She quickly looked around, wondering if there was some sort of view the prophet was enjoying, but their surroundings were just as foggy as ever. What a weirdo.

"I've been awaiting you," Malan said without wasting time on greetings. "You're late."

"Late for what?" Cam asked, vocalising what Macey was just about to ask.

"Dinner. I had to eat it all by myself."

Macey and Jared exchanged a worried look.

"What did you have?" Macey asked tentatively.

"Waffles, of course."

The look of devastation on Jared's face was priceless, and Macey couldn't help but laugh, despite her own feelings of disappointment. Maybe Malan was just teasing them. She couldn't imagine him eating anyway; how was he supposed to get the food to his mouth without a body? There was no stomach either, nor all the other essential parts to process a meal. No, it had to have been a joke.

Malan hovered into the house, the door opening as if by magic. Who was she kidding, of course it was magic.

They followed him into the kitchen - why did he need a kitchen in the first place? - where he stopped and looked at them all with a serious expression, enhanced by his drawn together eyebrows, as bushy as ever.

"As I said, you're late. I can see the magic leaking from you, Macey, and you'd be well advised to get it under control before it's too late."

"What?" was all Macey could come up with.

"Have you had any extreme things happen to you recently? Has your magic spiralled out of control?" His tone was dripping with sarcasm, as if he was fully aware of what had occurred in the pool.

"Well, yes, but Rónán said-"

"Oh yes, the selkie." Malan turned in the air until he was staring right at Rónán. "You've got it wrong, boy."

Rónán frowned, but kept his composure. Macey admired that - and she was totally going to call him 'boy' later on to tease him.

"How do you even know what I said?" he asked, raising an eyebrow. "And what exactly am I wrong about?"

"You think the Great Orca is a legend. Well, he isn't. At least, not anymore."

It took Macey a moment to understand. "Wait, the orca that's supposed to represent the devil in Selkie legend?"

"Exactly that. But like every legend that many people believe in, it has created a vacuum in the shape of the being they've immortalised in their tale. Now, a creature is inhabiting that space and has become the Great Orca."

"Just like the Mahoun and Self-Doubt?" Macey asked.

"Exactly like them. It's yet another of their siblings. Right now, it's swimming towards the home of the selkies. If you want to save your kind, Rónán, you better head there now."

Malan's expression had changed, becoming almost sad, regretful. "I had a selkie friend once... never mind. I'd suggest you go there before you try taking on the Mahoun or someone else. The Great Orca will only grow in strength the more people see him and start believing in him. Once he's destroyed the selkies, he will go after the na fir ghorma next, and then the kelpies. You need to hurry."

"Do we have time?" Cam asked. "We're thinking the Mahoun is planning to do something to the earth, poisoning it. We can't let that happen either."

Malan nodded in his bodiless way. "I suggest you split up. Jared and Flint might want to travel to Earth, maybe taking the other two Wardens with them. Cam, Macey and Rónán can deal with the Orca."

"Who made you the one giving us orders?" Flint asked heatedly, but one look from Macey shut him up.

"He's right, Flint. You don't want to fight a water being, and we need Jared on Earth. This way, we all do what we're best suited to. We'll join you as soon as we've defeated the Orca."

"No, the sea is exactly where I'm needed," Flint replied angrily. "My fire will be much more effective against him than your water."

Macey frowned, remembering their earlier conversation.

"I agree. I think I need to go with Jared," she said.

"Why?" her incubus demanded. "Don't get me wrong, I always want you with me. But..."

"I don't know," Macey replied. "I just know that when I think about it, I know going with Jared is the right idea."

"I don't think..." Cam started.

"That ignoring her is a good idea?" Malan interrupted, a crooked smile on his transparent face.

Macey tried not to get too freaked out by the man's face. But he was weird and she didn't know how to properly deal with him.

"Maybe not," Cam admitted.

"See," Macey said, sticking out her tongue in a surprisingly childish mood. After so long in captivity and being in high stress situations, she could take a moment to regress a little. It wasn't like it was going to scare off any of her men. She was pretty sure they were with her for good.

"I'm not exactly going to complain," Jared said with an impish grin. "Maybe while we're at it, we can give me a top up." He winked.

"It's settled then." Malan announced. "Flint, Rónán and Cam will head for the sea and the Great Orca, while Macey and Jared head beneath the earth to check everything is running smoothly. And all in time for a spot of tea."

Macey gaped at the prophet. How was he even going to drink it? It baffled her every time he mentioned food and drink. He seemed to be so obsessed with it, yet there was no way for him to even ingest it.

"You don't want to know," Cam whispered in her ear.

"What?" she returned.

"How he eats and drinks. You don't want to know."

She nodded once, accepting his words as true.

"So what's the plan?" she asked her men, ignoring the floating prophet. "I mean, we need one of you who can travel the Staran to take us to earth, right?" She looked between Flint and Cam, wondering which of them would respond to her first.

Jared laughed heartily. "Oh little kelpie, we don't need the Staran to get where we're going."

"We don't?"

"Not at all."

SEVEN

After a hug with Flint, Cam and Rónán – all of them took a long time to let her go – Jared led her outside, into what could be described as the prophet's front garden. She grinned when she saw the bench once again. Malan was so strange that it was almost endearing.

"Why are you smiling?" Jared enquired.

Macey shrugged. "Just... Malan."

He winked. "Yes, he's rather special. He can be terrifying though if you're not on his side. He's fought in wars before, and yes, I know how weird that is. His powers are legendary, even considering his lack of a body. I guess it makes him less easy to hit in battle."

He walked a few more steps away from the house and kneeled on the misty ground. Macey couldn't even spot what they were walking on, but she assumed it was Earth, judging from the way Jared's eyes began to glow in magical delight. He didn't have the chance to use his magic often, less so than the other guys. His powers were too volatile, too damaging.

When nothing happened after half a minute of him kneeling on the ground, his hands touching the earth, Macey asked, "What are you doing exactly?"

"Shhhh."

She grimaced and continued to wait. Jared didn't move, not even averting his gaze from the ground. Was there something he could see and she couldn't?

After three minutes or so, the question of what they were waiting for threatened to burst from her lips. Last time she'd seen him use his magic, he'd lowered them into the earth back on St Kilda, it had been quick, not like this.

It was boring.

The others had probably reached the ocean already. Why couldn't Macey and Jared travel on the Staran? It was so much easier, especially now that the pathways had been healed.

"I can sense your impatience," Jared muttered. "Relax. I'm almost there."

"Almost where?"

"You'll see," he murmured and went back to staring at the mist beneath them.

Macey looked back at the prophet's house. Was

Malan looking at them through the windows? She bet he was. They had to look completely incompetent from a distance.

Suddenly, the ground shook and Macey whipped around to look at Jared – who was now sunk halfway into the earth, only his torso looking out.

"What. The. Waves?" She clutched at his arms, pulling at them, trying to get Jared out of his predicament, but she stopped when he began to laugh loudly.

"Stop, that hurts," he joked. "This is what's supposed to happen. We're going to travel through the earth, that way we'll know if something is wrong straight away."

"Wait. We're travelling through the earth? How are we going to breathe?"

"I've made us a tunnel. I hope you're not claustrophobic."

"Wait," she repeated. "How is a tunnel from this place going to connect us to Earth? That's impossible!"

He grinned widely. "Nothing is impossible. But you're right, it's not a physical tunnel as such. It's metaphysical, an abstract concept that is turning into reality by my magic holding it in place."

"What?"

"It would take too long to explain. Just trust me that this will get us back to Earth. If I've calculated correctly, we might even be able to get some real Belgian waffles at the end of our journey."

Macey stared at him, not quite sure about the whole thing. Were they really going to travel *through* the earth? That was so impossible that she was beginning to think he was playing with her. Only one way to find out.

"Let's go," she said far more confidently than she felt. "What do I do?"

"I'm going to lower myself further down and then you'll climb into the tunnel. I'll keep hold of your feet so you'll know you're still with me. Don't worry, I won't let you become lost."

"How long is it going to take?"

"Maybe an hour, maybe longer. I don't usually take other people with me when I travel this way, so I'm going to need to use more magic."

Macey put her hands on her hips and glared at him, just to make sure he got how unhappy she was with this mode of travel. "Promise me I won't suffocate?"

He chuckled. "I promise. You'll be safe as mud."

She wrinkled her brow. "Is that an Earth mage saying?"

"Nope, just a Jared expression. Besides, if you suffocate, I'll just have to give you the kiss of life. Now, are you ready?"

Macey took a deep breath and approached her incubus. "I guess I am."

"Good. Once I'm lower down, just sit on the side of the hole and I'll pull you down."

"Do you know how creepy this is? It's usually in horror films that people get dragged into the ground."

"I'll keep you safe." His eyes met hers and she was struck by the warmth and confidence in his gaze. Yes, he really was going to keep her safe.

Slowly, he sank into the earth as if pulled by an unseen rope. She gasped when his head disappeared, but then hurried to sit on the side of the hole like he'd instructed. She gasped again when he wrapped his hands around her ankles, even though she'd expected it. This had to be the weirdest thing she'd ever done.

Macey took a deep breath, just in time because a moment later, Jared pulled on her legs and she slid off the ledge and into the dark, deep tunnel he'd created.

She closed her eyes to prevent any earth from getting into them, and tried to breathe as shallow as possible. The air in the tunnel smelled funny but not unpleasant. It reminded her of nutmeg and paprika powder.

There was a strange kind of buffer between her and the tunnel walls, like an air cushion, preventing her skin from chafing and her clothes from getting dirty. She had a newfound respect for Jared's powers. This was incredible. Magical.

After a few minutes, when she was sure that no earth was going to hit her face, she dared to open her eyes – and grinned when she didn't see anything but darkness. She should have known that. At least it was more comfortable to keep her eyes open.

Time passed slowly. She tried calling out to Jared, but it seemed that they couldn't hear each other. It was completely silent in the tunnel; the only sound was her breath. The barrier surrounding her seemed to muffle all sounds, especially that of them rushing through the earth.

The darkness made her tired and she let her mind drift off into daydreams of her other men, on their way to fight the Orca. Strange how she counted all three of them as her men, even Rónán. He fit so well into their dynamic that she had trouble imagining that he'd only just joined them. She was so lucky to have such amazing guys.

She smiled. She really was one lucky kelpie.

"REMIND me why we've never used this before?" she asked once they'd made the excruciatingly long journey.

"It wasn't working before."

"Right...and it's safe now because..."

Jared didn't respond immediately. Instead, he paced around where they'd landed.

Damn. She should have gone to the sea. At least there she'd know what she was up against. Water was her element after all. She could deal with it in her sleep. Past drowning experience notwithstanding.

"I didn't have the energy before," he admitted. "But being with you has recharged me enough."

"Reassuring," she muttered.

Jared chuckled and turned to her. Leaning down, he pressed his lips against hers and kissed her gently. Their lips moved in tandem, a warmth spreading through her body at the touch. Maybe whatever had caused the scales really had made it so she needed to devour men now. .

"Stop thinking about it, we got here safely," Jared mumbled against her lips, his hot breath fanning against them and setting every nerve on fire.

"I can't," she replied as she stepped back and broke their kiss. "Something's changed, Jared."

He frowned at her. "And you think you're turning into an incubus?" He raised an eyebrow.

"Wouldn't it be like a succubus?" she prompted, genuinely curious.

"Technically not, we're different in a couple of ways." He shrugged as if it wasn't all that important.

"Alright then." She paused, trying to compose the

thoughts in her head so she could actually express them. "I don't think I'm turning into an incubus. But there does seem to be some kind of hunger I didn't have before."

"A sexual one?"

"I'm not sure." She grimaced, not at all happy with the vagueness of her own words. "I don't think so. But I'm also not sure what it is."

"Could it be magic?"

"What?" she snapped.

"A hunger for magic and power," he clarified.

"I..." She glanced away from him, unable to stand the empathy in his dark eyes.

"We'll figure it out, Macey." He stepped forwards and cupped her face in one of his hands, lifting her chin slightly so their eyes met. "We love you. All of us. We'll figure out what's going on inside you and we'll do our best to make it right."

"I love you too. All of you." And she loved how he'd included the others, even if they weren't actually there with them anymore.

"Exactly. Now, let's get going and we can sort out inner-Macey later."

"Inner-Macey?" She snorted without meaning to. "Are you seriously going to call it that?"

"It's what makes the most sense." Jared shrugged. "Now, after you." He waved towards the path they'd landed next to.

"No way. We go together, or I'm staying here."

"You were the one who insisted on coming with me," Jared pointed out, a smug note in his voice.

"Stop being right," she muttered.

Jared held out his hand and she took it, enjoying the warm feel of his skin against hers. In all the daydreams she'd had while living in the Loch, this hadn't been one of them. None of this had. And while the bad things weren't exactly great, the good that came with it was definitely worth it.

"You do know where we're going, right?" she asked him.

"Of course."

"Care to enlighten me?" she prompted after he chose to ignore her for a moment.

"How familiar are you with Belgian geography?" Jared sounded amused and she was tempted to stop walking and cross her arms to get him to pay proper attention to her.

"Not at all. Are you trying to tell me…"

"That we're in Belgium? Yes."

"But why?"

"I have some friends here."

"Other incubi?" she asked after a pause.

"No. I don't really know any other incubi."

"Then how do you know how to use your powers?" She frowned, trying to imagine how she'd have managed as a youngling without older kelpies to teach her what to do. Basically, she wouldn't have gotten anywhere.

"Trial and error." Jared shrugged as he carried on walking. "For my incubi powers anyway. The people we're going to see now are who taught me how to work with earth."

"People?"

"You're full of questions today," Jared teased.

"I wonder why," she muttered.

"We're going to see the kabouter."

"Bless you?" Macey frowned in confusion.

Jared laughed. "No, ca-bow-ter," he said slowly. "Gnomes," he added when he noticed her confused face.

"Then why didn't you just say that?"

"Do you like being called a mythical water horse?"

Macey pouted but conceded the point. She just wanted to kick something whenever anyone used that to describe her.

"And the kabouter taught you how to control the earth?"

"Yes. I seemed to attract them the moment my powers manifested. They're big fans of mudslides."

"That's how your powers manifested?" Her lips pulled up at the side as she tried and failed to smother a laugh.

"And how did yours manifest?" he asked,

attempting to sound stern. The laughter was bubbling up in him too though. She could sense it.

"I was born a kelpie," she replied. "We know what we are the moment we're born."

"And your water powers?" he prompted.

Macey frowned as she tried to recall the moment she'd first done magic. "I made a small whirlpool that ripped my brothers' clothes." She smiled to herself at the memory, before recalling how trapped her brothers were.

"We'll get them back." Jared slipped an arm around her as they walked and squeezed her to him.

"I'm starting to doubt that."

"We will." Even as down as she was, she could hear the doubt in his voice. She appreciated what he was trying to do and knew all of them would try their best to free them.

"I know we'll try," she acknowledged. "But will we actually succeed? There's another question."

"Hmm."

They lapsed into silence as they walked.

Kabouter

EIGHT

Jared brought them to a halt in front of a collection of tiny mushrooms on the forest floor. He leaned down and began to almost tickle the fungi, a smile lighting up his face.

"Did you eat some of these?" Macey asked, trying not to laugh. Her mood had lifted substantially since walking through the woods. There was something magical about it. Haunting even. And the beauty had chased away some of her inner demons.

"No," Jared replied. He rose to his feet, chuckling away before speaking words Macey didn't understand.

Before her eyes, the earth began to peel backwards, leaving two great hills topped with mushrooms and what seemed like a stone staircase leading into the earth between them. The whole transition must have only taken a few seconds, and she was once again in awe of the wonders magic could achieve.

"I take it that's where we're going?"

"You got it." Jared placed a hand on the small of her back and guided her to the stone stairway.

Carefully, she placed one foot after the other. The last thing she wanted was to fall down and break something. Or make an ass out of herself in front of the kabouters.

The moment their heads were lower than the earth, it began to close in on itself, darkening their path and making the way more difficult. Much to Macey's delight, a couple more steps revealed glowing jewels in the sides of the walls, allowing her to see once more.

"It's beautiful," she gasped as she really took it in. There were gems of all different shapes, sizes and colours, and the lights they created were dancing across the stairway and down into the depths.

"They really are. The kabouters take great pride in their pathways."

"I can see why."

Macey was at least a little surprised by how free she felt. The earth always sounded so claustrophobic and not at all like the open water she was used to.

"Jared!" a little girl's voice screamed.

From the corner of her eye, she spotted a blur firing itself at Jared, who just laughed as he caught it.

"Gisella!" he cried. "How are you doing?"

"Well," the little girl answered. She was wearing what Macey could only describe as a blue pinafore dress with a checked shirt underneath and a pointy red hat. She hated thinking it but the little girl was every stereotypical thing she'd expect from a gnome. Other than being female, anyway.

"Is your grandpa in?" Jared asked.

"Yes, should I take you to him?"

"Please."

Gisella squirmed in Jared's arms and he set her down on the floor. She trotted off into the distance, leaving the two adults to follow.

"How come I can understand her?" Macey asked.

"I wondered if you'd notice that." Jared chuckled. "It's something to do with the magic of this place. Everything is translated to the hearer's natural tongue. Even childlike language is basically non-existent. This place just changes it into what is meant."

"Wow. Magic..."

"Is pretty cool, right?" He grinned widely at her.

"Are all the kabouter like..." she waved in front of her at Gisella rather than voicing the words.

"Short? Yes. They're pretty much like they are in your culture, but you know... Flemish."

"And I shouldn't call them by their other names," Macey finished for him. "Got you. Anything else I should know?"

"I don't think so." Jared shrugged. "But I'm not sure. I can't say I've ever brought a water being here before."

"Reassuring," Macey muttered.

"Jared!" a voice boomed. "You finally brought a girlfriend for us to meet." The man in front of them was a quintessential gnome as far as Macey could tell, even down to the wide grin on his face as he studied her incubus.

"Jerimiah," Jared acknowledged, dipping his head in respect..

Jared turned to Macey with a wide grin.

"Meet Jerimiah, crown prince of the kabouters, son of King Kyrië, and father to lovely Gisella." He tickled the little girl's neck and she squealed in delight.

Yet another royal, Macey thought as she smiled at the gnome.

"It's a pleasure, Jerimiah," she said pleasantly, wondering whether she should announce her titles as well. But in the end, they didn't really matter. Nobody here would care that she was a kelpie princess.

The gnome laughed heartily. "Don't be so formal, little one. Any friend of Jared's is welcome here."

"Little one?" Macey mouthed to Jared who was visibly trying not to laugh.

"He's not talking about size, he's talking about

age," he whispered. "Kabouters can be centuries old, and I think Jerimiah is close to two hundred."

That made more sense, but still, Macey couldn't get over the fact that a gnome whose long hat barely reached her chest had called her 'little'.

"Come, come, follow me," Jerimiah called and ran off with the same energy his daughter had shown earlier. Jared chuckled and began to run, leaving Macey to follow him. She would have loved to walk along the beautiful corridors and admire the gem-crusted walls some more, but apparently, kabouters loved running at a neckbreaking pace.

She was out of breath by the time they reached a cosy, warm cave, the walls sparkling with rubies and garnets. The furniture was a mixture of fur covered stones and simple wooden shelves, which made it all even more comfy looking. It was a home, not just a random cave.

"Sit, sit," the Kabouter prince encouraged them, pointing to a sofa in the middle of the room. "Smal! We have guests! Make some tea, will you?"

Before they were even seated, a tiny gnome appeared from another tunnel entrance, her long brown hair almost reaching the floor. She had a perfect hourglass figure and instead of a hat, she was wearing a yellow cap, matching her amber eyes. For a kabouter, she was extremely pretty.

"Smal, my wife," Jerimiah introduced her. "Do we still have some of the dandelion root tea, darling?"

Smal wasn't listening though, she was hugging Jared who was looking at Macey with a sheepish expression, as if to say that the embrace wasn't his idea. He gently patted her back while she gripped him tight.

When she stepped back, her expression turned from a wide smile to a stern glare. "Don't you ever stay away this long again without sending word," she admonished Jared. "I've been worried sick."

He blushed. "It's not been all that long," he defended himself. "Maybe a year?"

Smal put her hands on her hips and her glare increased. "Fifteen months. Fif-teen months, young man. That's at least fourteen months too many."

"I was busy," Jared muttered, looking at Macey for help. She just grinned innocently, enjoying the show. She was beginning to like this Kabouter family.

"Stop it, Smal," Jerimiah said and pulled his wife away from the incubus. "Go, make some tea, and maybe get some biscuits. Our boy looks like he could do with some food."

Smal turned her glare at her husband, but then did as he'd asked, hurrying off into yet another tunnel.

Finally, Macey and Jared sat down on the sofa. The incubus looked relieved now that he was no longer being hugged or admonished by the female gnome. Good, Macey had started to feel sorry for him. Little Gisella seemed to think the same, because as soon as they'd sat down, she jumped on Jared's lap, making herself comfortable. Her hat tickled his chin and he gently readjusted the girl's position.

He would make a good dad, Macey thought, before stopping herself from imagining Jared holding several of his own children on his lap. Hopefully, there wasn't going to be a baby any time soon; they had a world to save first.

Which is what had brought them here, after all.

"I assume this isn't just a family visit to introduce us to your girlfriend?" Jerimiah asked, sitting on an armchair opposite them that seemed to be made from roots twisted tightly together.

"You know him," Smal scoffed, returning with a tray of steaming mugs. "He only comes when he needs something. He's never got time for his mama anymore."

"Mama?" Macey whispered.

"They kind of see me as their adopted son," Jared muttered under his breath. He lifted his voice. "I wanted to visit but then I met Macey and..."

Smal's expression immediately lightened. "And you only had eyes and ears for her," she finished his sentence. "Of course, we understand, don't we, Jemmy?"

Her kabouter husband flinched at her public use of his nickname and Macey had to stifle a grin. They seemed like such an adorable couple.

"Gisella, I think it's time for you to go to bed," he said to his daughter instead, and after some complaining, the little kabouter ran off, presumably to her bedcave.

Jared coughed. "Well, yes, and Macey got kidnapped and it took me a while to find her again. And now..."

"You let your girlfriend get kidnapped?" Smal screeched and jabbed her small index finger towards Jared. "How is she still with you?"

Macey shrugged. "I rescued myself, Jared never got the chance to free me. I'm sure he would have done a great job otherwise."

"Of course he would have," Smal nodded enthusiastically and pressed a mug of tea in Macey's hands. "We raised him. He'd have been your Prince Charming if only you'd let him."

Was the kabouter telling her off for not staying in the Voice's dungeons long enough for Jared to rescue her? This was getting weirder every minute.

"We're here because..." Jared began again, but the gnome woman interrupted him.

"Is she pregnant?"

"What?! No! Of course not," Macey spluttered. She wasn't even sure if she could get pregnant on land. Most kelpies reproduced in kelpie form, it made the foaling easier.

"That's neither here nor there," Jared muttered, his already dark skin growing darker in his embarrassment.

"Having troubles then?" Smal asked, a knowing smile on her face. "I know just the thing for that."

Before either of them could say anymore, the kabouter was running out of the room and towards whatever it was she had in mind.

"Sorry," Jared muttered.

Rather than answering aloud, Macey placed a reassuring hand on his arm, knowing he'd understand what she meant by it.

"She's just excited about the possibility of babies," Jerimiah explained. "There haven't been any born here in a while."

"There haven't?" Jared seemed surprised. "Why?"

"I don't know." The kabouter glanced away, a sorrowful look on his face. "But for the past year, not one of the women has been able to conceive. It's the same across the world."

"A year?" Macey whispered, counting back the months in her head. Depending how long she'd been in the Voice's care, it'd only been three or four months since their quest to save the Staran had started. Certainly not that long.

"Yes. At first, we thought it was just a timing thing. Now..."

"Now it seems more purposeful," Jared finished for him.

"It's certainly not right. But we're not sure what the cause of it is."

Macey exchanged glances with Jared, who shook his head slightly. She nodded, there was no use scaring the people he considered family with what had happened to the Staran. It was their issue to sort.

"That's sort of why we're here," Jared started. "I've been getting this feeling like there's something wrong with the earth."

"Ah, you've felt it too. I wasn't sure with you living in the mists."

"Yes, it's only been faint for now, but it's gotten stronger," Jared explained.

"Worrying," the kabouter mused.

"Do you have any idea what's going on?" Macey asked, hoping they had at least some answers.

"No, but the kludde have been getting restless. They've made others very wary of going near the water."

"Kludde?"

"Tricksters. They like to lure humans to certain death and destruction. I suppose they're not unlike your Scottish kelpies in their murderous intent," the kabouter said cheerfully.

Macey bristled, hating the bad reputation of her kind. Jared's firm hand gave her knee a reassuring squeeze. Maybe she shouldn't get too angry. She didn't want them to think even worse of her.

"I found it!" Smal interrupted the awkwardness by hurrying back in with something shiny in her hands and a triumphant grin lighting up her face. "Here." She passed the glittering object to Macey who took it reverently.

Holding it up to the light, the pendant glittered, revealing intricate swirls of thinly cut strips of gemstones. It twirled around in the light, reflecting off the gems. "It's beautiful."

"Just like you." Smal grinned at her.

Macey blushed. Beautiful wasn't something she'd considered herself up until meeting her men. In kelpie terms she was kind of plain. When it came to human ideals of beauty, she supposed she was pretty at most. But it was hard to tell when she was looking at herself. It was only when her men's eyes were on her that she truly felt beautiful. There was something about the reverent way they looked at her that spoke straight to her soul.

"Well, put it on," Smal insisted.

Jared took the necklace from her and looped it around her neck, making sure he moved her hair out of the way first. With each brush of his fingers over her skin, Macey trembled and wished they were alone. Maybe that was Smal's plan. Make her so turned on that she had too much sex not to get pregnant.

She frowned to herself. Incubi were rare, even Jared said so, but why? They were all about sex and needed a lot of it to survive, so surely babies should be common. Unless they took on the characteristics of their mothers.

"It's very hard for an incubus to have a child," Jared whispered in her ear as he clasped the necklace.

"How do you..."

"Your body language," he answered. "And I know you. Your mind is far too curious not to wonder."

"Oh."

He leaned back before she could say anything else and she knew the conversation was done for now. They could pick it up later when there was actually time to discuss children and how it would work with four potential fathers. Hopefully she wouldn't add anyone else into the mix, though six did seem like a good family number.

Macey shook her head, ridding herself of the thoughts that entailed. It was bad enough she had four men, she didn't need more than that. No woman did.

"What does it do?" Macey asked Smal, while fingering the pendant.

"It's for luck," Smal responded. "Not specifically

for babies, mind. But it'll do the job just as well as any fertility charm."

Macey hoped not. Though maybe it'd do the opposite just as well too. If she didn't want to get pregnant, then it could stop that. Dragging a baby around while they were on a mission to save the Staran wasn't the best of ideas.

"Thank you," she said earnestly, appreciating the present even if it wasn't quite for the reasons the other woman intended.

"Are you done, dear?" Jerimiah asked, his voice filled with adoration for his wife. If Macey didn't have her men, she might have been jealous of the bond the two of them clearly shared.

"Yes, yes, just making sure we get grandchildren."

Jared choked a little, but managed to cover it up with a fake sneeze.

"We have several hundred years for that, don't go rushing him the moment he meets a pretty woman."

"Hmmm." The kabouter woman crossed her arms, clearly not as sure as her husband was.

"We were talking about the kludde," Jared prompted, hopefully getting the conversation back on track.

"Ah yes, the kludde." Jerimiah grew serious again. "The water kludde are not letting anyone get close to their waters, as if they see everybody as a threat. Usually it's them doing the attacking, so I don't know what they could be afraid of. The earth kludde are similarly upset. They usually come out of their holes at twilight and dawn to do their tricks on travellers, but they've been reclusive for months now. The only ones I've seen are the ones we occasionally trade with, and they've not been forthcoming with information about what's going on."

"Wait, there's water and earth kludde?" Macey asked, confused. How was a horse shifter supposed to live in the ground?

"Of course," Jerimiah answered, "they're not bound to one shape. In the water, they turn into horses, but their cousins in the ground can take other forms. Often, they disguise themselves as trees to waylay travellers and rob them. But I've even heard of air kludde transforming into birds."

Macey was almost relieved to hear that these strange beings weren't like kelpies after all. Maybe they even looked like boring normal horses in the water, without pretty scales and webbed hooves.

The kabouter turned to Jared. "You said you felt a change. Why did you come here? There are places where you can be closer to the earth."

Macey frowned, but didn't comment. How were they supposed to get closer to the earth than being *inside* a cave underground?

"This is where I learned about my magic," Jared shrugged. "You and your family taught me everything

I know. I thought you might be able to help me once again, solving this mystery. " He took a deep breath. "It's not just the earth, Jerimiah. At this very moment, friends of ours are fighting a new evil in the Scottish sea that's taken the form of a giant orca. Not long ago, we defeated a being that had fed on the Staran like a leech. And before that, Macey and a friend of ours were kidnapped by the Mahoun."

Smal gasped. "Isn't that the Celtic version of the devil?"

Jared nodded grimly. "It is. There's a group of beings, evil creatures that we don't have a name for yet, who possess spaces created by our imagination. The devil is the easiest example. So many people believe in him, but if he doesn't actually exist, a space is formed by the collective belief in it. These beings fill those gaps and turn into representations of the spaces."

The two kabouters looked at each other, equally speechless. Macey wasn't quite sure whether they thought it an outlandish theory, or whether they were shocked by how bad the situation was.

Eventually, Smal said slowly, "So if we all suddenly started to believe in the Big Bad Wolf, he would become alive? Possessed by these... these things?"

Macey nodded. "That's how we understand it, yes. We don't know how many people need to believe in something though for it to become a space these creatures can inhabit. The devil, that's a very big one. The one we killed was Self-Doubt, again, a big one. We're not sure which one is harming the earth."

Jerimiah stroked his long beard, his brows furrowed. "For now, all we kabouters feel is a strange new energy in the earth. It's interfering with our magic, but not much, just enough to be noticeable. I think the earth kludde may be more sensitive to the change, or they're more affected. If the water kludde are feeling it, then it must be strong indeed and not just affecting the earth directly."

"But what belief is there that the creature could have used?" his wife asked. "There aren't any earth spirits or gods we believe in, and the humans most certainly don't. How abstract are we thinking?"

"Self-Doubt was feeding on the staran because of the doubts many travellers have," Macey explained. "So maybe it's something people connect to the earth? Some kind of sentiment that a lot of us experience?"

"Love? Admiration? Life?" Jerimiah suggested, but Macey shook her head.

"Claustrophobia."

Jared's eyes brightened. "That could be it! I guess some people could feel that in water as well. But isn't that quite a generic fear, not something we believe in?"

"Well, Self-Doubt wasn't something as specific as

the Mahoun or the Orca," Macey countered. "But for now, we don't really need to know what it is; we need to know where it is so we can find and defeat it."

"We'll help however we can," Smal announced, and her husband nodded in agreement. "We can send messages to other kabouter families to see if they've noticed anything strange. Our tunnel network reaches most parts of Belgium and even into the Netherlands, so if something is happening in this country, we'll know soon."

She turned to Macey and gave her a very obvious wink. "You might like to retire to our guest room in the meantime, sweetie? Now that you have that necklace..."

Was Smal really suggesting that her and Jared were supposed to have sex so they could have grand-children? Now? In their home? Were all kabouters this strange?

Jared laughed in a strangled sort of way and got up, pulling Macey with him. "Is my old room still empty?"

Smal looked a little disappointed, but her smile returned immediately. "Yes, although it may be a bit small for the both of you..."

The incubus grinned. "It will be enough, don't worry. When do you think we'll have an answer from your network? Four hours? Five?"

"Three," Jerimiah proudly said. "We've improved

our communication channels since you left, boy. Every family now has-"

"Not now, darling," Smal interrupted her husband. "Let them get some rest."

From her smile, it was obvious that 'rest' didn't equal sleep in Smal's mind. To be honest, it didn't in Macey's either. She wasn't quite sure what time it was, but it couldn't be much later than early afternoon. Sleeping now just seemed like a waste of time, especially when she had the chance to be alone with Jared for a bit.

"See you later," she told the grinning kabouter woman, and let the incubus lead her outside into one of the tunnels.

NINE

"So this is where you grew up?" she asked as Jared drew her into a small cave dotted with glowing gemstones.

"Yes, maybe about a century ago, I spent a couple of years here being taught what I needed to know."

"Only a couple of years?" she asked, frowning.

"I've been back since. I pop in at least once a year." He smiled warmly at her.

"You really love them, don't you?"

"Of course, they're my family. Everyone loves family," Jared pointed out.

"Yes..." Macey replied, thinking of her own complicated family dynamic.

"It'll be okay," Jared said, pulling her close to him and holding her tightly.

Macey wasn't convinced by how right he was

about that, but if it meant he'd hold her like this then she was all for it. Saying that, she really did need to visit Aunt Nessie and discover the actual truth about her parentage. Only then would she be able to move forward with a family of her own.

"Hey, stop thinking about it so hard," Jared murmured, tipping back Macey's face so he could look into her eyes. "We'll figure it out together."

"I don't know why you want me when I come with so many complications," she responded, sniffing slightly as the tears threatened to fall.

"Because I love you," he replied, leaning down and pressing his lips gently against hers.

He started slow, increasing the pressure and the tempo as he went. Macey pushed her body into his, feeling the hard planes of him against her own softness. She moaned into the kiss and slipped her hand under the hem of Jared's shirt. He was quicker than she was and whipped the whole thing over his head, swiftly undressing the rest of them, throwing their clothes to the ground.

"In a hurry?" she teased after breaking their kiss.

"No more waiting, little kelpie. It's been too long since I was alone with you." There was an edge to his voice which she suspected meant his incubus nature was close to the surface. Anticipation thrummed through her. Sex with Jared was good. Sex with incubus Jared was even better.

Without saying a word, she dropped to her knees, looking up at Jared through her eyelashes. His eyes filled with hunger as he looked down on her, causing a sense of satisfaction to swiftly flow through her. She was the one making him like this. Her and no one else.

Leaning forward, her tongue darted out and she lapped at the top of his cock, keeping the pressure light and teasing. She didn't want this to be over too soon, so going a little slower than she wanted was the right option.

"Macey," Jared groaned.

Grinning, she changed tactics, taking his cock into her mouth and placing her hand at the base to stop him from hitting the back of her throat and causing her gag reflex to kick in. That wouldn't be a fun way to end their evening. Maybe in time she'd be able to take him further, but she had plans for him that didn't involve this being over quickly.

Jared's hands threaded through her hair, pulling her closer and controlling the movements of her head as she took his cock in and out of her mouth, dragging her lips against him and eliciting a series of moans and groans from him.

She let out a soft hum, which vibrated through the pair of them.

"I think that's enough now," Jared said through bated breaths.

He tugged on her hair and she tipped back, his cock leaving her mouth and standing proudly between them.

"Get on the bed," he said softly. It was different from the orders he'd given the first time they'd been alone together. There wasn't anything quite so demanding about it. There was an emotion behind it which hadn't existed quite so clearly before.

Macey got to her feet and made the short trip to the bed. Knowing what Jared liked, she began to lie down on her front.

"Not tonight," Jared countered. "Lie on your back."

She complied, lying across the bed naked and exposed. Jared closed the distance between them and sank down onto the bed next to her, the mattress dipping as he did.

"I want to be able to look into your eyes this time."

Macey's heart filled to bursting and her eyes glazed over as the affection and lust combined to create a whole new sensation.

Jared leaned forward and began to trace lines over her stomach. Macey glanced down and noticed he was following the patterns caused by the shining gemstones off the wall. His eyes looked on at her with reverent feeling.

"You're beautiful."

"Kiss me," she whispered, needing more from him.

Jared complied almost instantly, placing himself above her and making her wish he was pressing her into the bed. Macey reached up and cupped his face, stroking a thumb over his cheek as they stared into one another's eyes.

After a few moments, Jared leaned down and kissed her tenderly. His body lowered closer to hers and sparks engulfed Macey where their naked skin touched. There really was nothing like this. No way of feeling so loved, cherished and needed.

His lips moved from hers and travelled down her neck, leaving fluttery sensations in their wake as he reached her collarbone.

"Switch with me," he murmured against her, the words vibrating against her skin.

It took her a second to realise what he meant, but obediently moved so he could take her place lying on the bed. Without wasting any more time, she resumed their kiss, very conscious of the hard cock brushing against the inside of her thigh. While she wanted him, she didn't want to rush him. Or this. They had a little bit of time, and right now, they were creating a memory they could treasure.

Slowly, she lowered herself down on to him, letting him fill her completely. The two of them set their own rhythm, the movements slow and sensual.

Macey lost track of time as they continued their private dance, each of them growing closer to the climax with each single stroke until it became too much.

Crying out, Macey reached her release and Jared joined her seconds later.

He hugged her tight as the final shivers of their release ran through them.

"That was magnificent," Jared muttered, but Macey didn't want to hear how it had been. She wanted more. She wanted to make it even more magnificent than he thought possible.

His cock still inside her, she began to sway her hips, leaving Jared's embrace so she could sit up and ride him.

"What are you doing?" he asked, but she didn't reply. It was obvious, and his cock decided the same, springing back to life, growing hard within her.

She wrapped her legs around his thighs, tightening her hold on him, binding her pelvis to his. Her breasts were whipping up and down as she rode him and his eyes were fixed on her chest, need and desire burning within them. He stretched out his hands and encompassed her breasts, massaging them roughly as she continued to fuck him.

Yes, there was no other word for it. She was in charge, she was making both of them feel good, just like she'd taken charge earlier when she sucked his cock. Was this a new side to her, caused by the weird 'man devouring' desire, or had it always been slumbering beneath the surface and now came out through Jared's incubus powers?

"Your scales," Jared suddenly said and his eyes widened. "You have scales."

She looked down at herself, admiring the faint covering of miniscule scales that had taken over the skin on her legs and arms. They were rapidly spreading, like a rash but much more beautiful, covering her belly and chest. She could feel the skin of her breasts harden beneath Jared's fingers, and that almost drove her over the edge.

"That happened before with Rónán," she explained, never stopping her rhythmical movements. She was getting close and there was no way she was going to cease without getting her second release. "They disappeared again though after we had... sex."

She wasn't sure how much information Jared wanted. Sure, he'd felt their sexual energy and knew very well what the selkie and her had been up to, but the whole dynamic of being with four men and all of them being okay with that, was still new to her. Waves, it was new to all of them.

"You're changing," Jared mused but it came out as a groan as Macey increased her rhythm. "I think I like this new you. You're more intense. Feral."

"Feral?!" She jerked her pelvis forward abruptly,

signalling him that she did not approve of his choice of words.

"More kelpie while you're human," he explained, taking his hands off her breasts and pushing her pelvis back until she was sitting perfectly on his cock again. "Maybe you're more human while you're kelpie, too."

Jared suddenly grinned. "Stop," he groaned and Macey complied in confusion. Didn't he want her anymore now that she had scales?

He lifted her off him as easily as if she weighed nothing, and rolled her onto her back, before spreading her legs and kneeling in between them.

"I want to see where else you have scales," he said, his voice full of heated desire.

She smiled, then moaned as his tongue explored her. He expertly licked over the sensitive skin, flicking his tongue against that precise point that made her shiver and want to come.

He ended far too soon and resurfaced, grinning. "Yes, you've got scales there too. Tiny ones, though. Exquisite. They're all shiny now that you're aroused. I think I need to lick them again to make sure they're real."

She returned his grin. "Yes, I think you should."

He spread her legs a little further and continued his exploration, his tongue finding ever new spots that made Macey quiver and moan. The scales seemed to make her even more sensitive to his touch, and it wasn't long until she had to beg him to stop.

"Get inside me," she said hoarsely, need lacing her voice. "I need you inside of me."

"Are there scales-"

"Don't."

He grinned but did as she'd asked, driving his cock into her with one fluid motion.

"I'm not going to last long," she moaned. Her nerves felt like they were full of electricity, making her skin tingle every time Jared touched her. His hands landed on her breasts again, squeezing her nipples.

"Your eyes are glowing," he whispered, and for some reason, that drove her over the edge. Her hands gripped the bed sheet as the orgasm ripped through her, while Jared continued to press into her, groaning with desire.

She met his eyes and saw the flecks of gold flashing in them when he came inside of her, his incubus powers feeding on their combined energy. He stayed in the same position for a moment and she savoured the feeling of him, still large and thick in her, not wanting it to end. Was she really this insatiable now that two times weren't enough?

He bent down to kiss her and she met his lips with hers. A shiver ran over her body, more than just goosebumps. It felt strange and she broke the kiss to look at her arms.

The scales were gone.

"You're pretty with scales and without," Jared whispered, claiming her lips again. She smiled and returned the kiss, pouring as much love and adoration into the kiss as she could.

MACEY CRINGED at the knowing smile Smal gave them when they returned to the living cave. They'd had a quick nap to regain their strength, but now Macey was hungry and they'd decided to rejoin the kabouters.

"Any news yet?" Jared asked.

"Jerimiah is talking to his contacts just now," the kabouter woman explained. "He might be another few minutes. I made you some dinner. You need to eat more, dear, you're thin as a stick." That last sentence was aimed at Macey, who was having a hard time not to laugh. She wasn't a stick exactly, unless the stick had curves and boobs.

Jared sniffed the air and his eyes widened slightly. "Do I smell waffles?"

Smal laughed. "Of course. How could I not make your favourite dish when you finally come to visit again. First, some soup though, you need some vitamins."

The incubus sighed. "I could eat some fruit with the waffles to get those."

The kabouter put her hands on her hips and stared him down. "No, veggies first, then you can have your waffles."

Macey suppressed a grin. Smal was treating him like a boy despite the fact that he was over a century old. Oh well, if they had to eat soup to get waffles, that was fine by her.

Smal disappeared into one of the tunnels and returned moments later with a steaming pot. She'd already decked the table in the centre of the cave and Macey sat down, hunger spreading through her stomach.

"Ella! Come eat!" Smal shouted, and Macey noticed a smaller bowl on the table, together with an intricately carved wooden spoon, half the size of her own. Cute.

The little kabouter girl came running into the cave, her hair tousled and specks of dirt on her face.

Smal sighed. "What did you do?"

Gisella shrugged. "Digging for earthworms. I thought James could do with a companion."

"James is her worm pet," Jared explained in a whisper. "Don't even ask."

"I wasn't going to," Macey muttered. Of all the

things she'd ever imagined asking someone, earth-worm relationships had never made the list. Maybe she should expand it to include such things now. That way she wouldn't end up taken aback like this.

"I have answers!" Jerimiah called, rushing back into the room.

Macey perked up. Answers were always good. Hopefully these would be more satisfying than those Malan or any of the others had given her.

"Go on," Jared prompted, taking a sip of his soup and slurping a little too much for Macey's liking. She elbowed him gently and he shot her an apologetic look.

"Is there any meat in this?" she asked him under her breath. She didn't want Smal to think she was rude, but she also didn't feel all that great about potentially breaking her vegetarian diet. Not only did she not like the taste but she wasn't all that convinced her stomach could deal with it.

"No," Jared answered instantly. "The earth kabouters are vegetarian, like you." He smiled at her, pure affection radiating off him.

"Great." She beamed back and took a big spoonful of her soup. It was delicious, the perfect combination of salt, spices and vegetables. It was almost as good as the idea of waffles.

"What news is there?" Jared prompted after a moment.

"There's a rumbling slightly to the east. Earthquakes mostly. I haven't heard this first hand, but there's allegedly been some eruptions from dormant volcanoes further south. It's not from the kabouters though, so I don't know the truth of it."

"And it's not just global warming?" Jared checked.

"I doubt it," Jerimiah answered. "Of course, that's what the humans are going to put it down to, but from what I've seen, that's their answer for everything going wrong."

Macey couldn't bring herself to disagree. She didn't think it was always the case, but she also didn't want to argue with her new quasi father-in-law.

"What can we do about it?" she asked.

"There probably isn't anything we can do," Smal said sadly, rubbing her daughter's back as she spoke. The little girl had started humming to herself as she doodled on a piece of paper, apparently ignoring her food. None of the adults seemed to care now, they were more focused on the matter at hand.

"There will be," Jared countered. "Macey already defeated Self-Doubt."

Her ears began to heat with embarrassment and she glanced away, unable to meet anyone's gaze. How could she when the two kabouters were looking at her in such awe.

"That may be right, but I don't think you'll find

the answers here," Jerimiah said. "I think it's time you go and see the kluddes."

"Alright, let's just have the waffles first," Jared joked. "Then I'll take her to the Meer."

"Good thinking," Smal said. "There isn't any need to rush quite yet." She grinned broadly.

They were finally going to get waffles. It had been so long, she'd started to doubt she'd ever get them. But it was all about to change.

They continued to eat their soup in silence, each of them lost in their own thoughts. Probably those of Belgian pastries, warm and dripping in butter.

A loud rumble started beneath them and the earth around them began to shake. A stream of dust rained down from the ceiling and scattered itself around the table, even dropping into their soup.

"On second thoughts, it might be best you go now." Jerimiah's voice shook as he spoke.

Disappointment filled Macey. Mostly because she knew the kabouter was right. Waffles would have to come later. She had a world to sort out first.

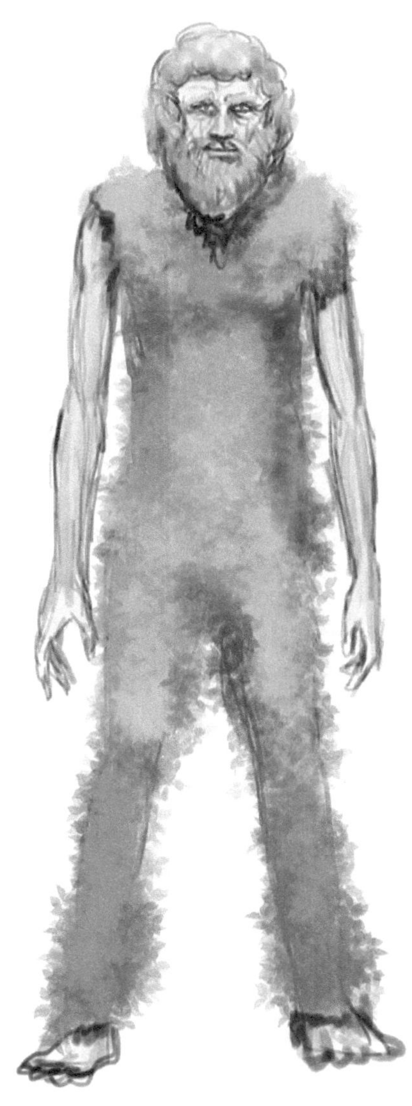

Kludde

TEN

"At least the mists make it feel like home," she mused as they walked towards the large lake Jerimiah had called the Meer. It loomed grey and mysterious in front of them.

Macey shuddered. She didn't know what to expect of the kludde. She hadn't even heard of them before coming to Belgium.

"Do you know how to find them?" she asked Jared.

"I don't think we find them, I think they find us."

"Reassuring." She sighed as they continued walking.

"Tell me more about them?"

Jared shrugged. "There's not much more I can really tell, I've never seen one myself so I have no idea what they're really like. All I know is that they like to play tricks on unwary travellers and can shift forms to do so."

"Like I can shift? Or..."

"Not quite like you. As far as I know, they can take any form they want. Within reason."

"And what would that reason be?" This was sounding less and less pleasant by the second. How were they even supposed to know if they were faced with one of the kludde if it could look like just about anything else when it stood in front of her.

"I don't think they can impersonate specific people." Jared shrugged again as if it was no big deal.

"You don't think?"

"Helllllllllllllo?" a voice called out through the mists.

Macey yelped and jumped backwards, surprised out of her skin by the sudden intrusion into their conversation.

"Hello?" she called back, her voice cracking with nerves. This wasn't the first impression she wanted to give to anyone, never mind the creatures they might want to ask for answers.

No response came. Macey took a deep breath and took another step into the mists, hoping whoever it was would make an appearance.

"Remind me why we're going to the water kludde and not the earth kludde?"

"They're easier to get to," Jared answered. "And less volatile."

"Worrying," Macey muttered to herself, but Jared's responding chuckle led her to believe he'd caught it. What damn crazy hearing the man must have.

"They just like to tease, Macey. Despite their reputation, I've never actually heard of a water kludde hurting anyone on purpose."

"But by accident?"

"Have you hurt anyone by accident?" he prompted.

She thought for a moment, then shivered, remembering the guards back at the Voice's keep. She had no idea if they'd actually been injured or not, but her intentions had certainly been there. Which was worse than hurting anyone by accident if anyone asked her. She'd actually purposefully tried to cause damage.

"Oh, no, Macey. I didn't mean it like that." Jared closed the small gap between them and pulled her into his arms, squeezing her tightly.

"I know you didn't," she responded, a morose note invading her voice. Whether he'd intended it or not, he'd put the thoughts into her head and there was no going back from that.

"You smell!" someone shouted, closer this time than the previous voice.

"Are they talking to us?" Macey asked Jared, turning around to try and spy whoever was moving through the mists.

"No idea. Maybe? It's a weird thing to say."

"No, they stink!" the first voice called from behind them.

It clearly seemed to be aimed at Macey and Jared.

"Are you the kludde?" she shouted, even though she really wanted to tell them that it was impolite to imply that they were smelly. But while the kludde didn't seem to care about first impressions, Macey did. They were in the kludde's territory now, and while Jared didn't seem to see them as much of a threat, the kelpie wasn't so sure about that.

"They positively reek," the second voice snick-ered, ignoring Macey's question. It sounded so close that Macey stretched out her hands and walked towards the sound, but there was nothing but mist in front of her.

"Come out so we can smell you!" she called in a burst of annoyance. "Then we can tell you if you stink as well."

Laughter sounded form all around her. There had to be at least ten or so people around them, but Macey couldn't see a single one.

"Glad that didn't make them angry," Jared whis-pered under his breath.

"Me too," Macey replied softly, her heart beating

a little faster. She lifted her voice to speak to the unseen strangers. "We're here to talk to the kludde about changes you may have noticed. We're fighting the evil that is..."

"Maybe she fights it with her smell," one voice interrupted her with a giggle and a chorus of laughter surrounded them once more.

"There was an earthquake not far from here today," Macey tried again. "Things are happening, bad things. If you haven't noticed anything, then tell us and we'll leave. We only want to help."

This time, there wasn't any laughter.

"Get Teacher," someone to her left whispered and the sound of running feet followed.

"Teacher?" Jared asked quietly so only Macey could hear. "Is that their leader, perhaps?"

"Maybe. Let's wait and find out."

They didn't have to wait long, for a minute later, a figure materialised in the mist a dozen yards or so before them.

"What is going on?" a booming voice asked.

Macey was just about to repeat her story when one of the younger voices replied, "Strangers are here, Teacher. We played with them but then one of them mentioned something about an earthquake and evil things, and..."

"What do you mean, played with them? You're

supposed to do your homework! Back to the classroom, now!"

There was shuffling all around them, indicating the kludde's departure. It was strange how Macey could see the Meer through the mist, but not the people they'd been talking to. Where they invisible?

"I apologise for my students," the deep voice said, suddenly right in front of them. But there was nothing. Absolutely nothing.

"Are you a ghost?" Macey blurted before she could stop herself.

"I am whatever I want to be," the Teacher replied. A second later, a horse stood on the marshy ground, so close Macey could feel its warm breath on her cheeks.

"Or maybe a dog?"

The horse changed into a large Rottweiler faster than the eye could see.

"Or a tree?"

A tree grew from the ground - no, it materialised, sprang into existence. Macey rubbed her eyes. Was this really happening? When she shifted, it took time and energy, and a dose of pain. This person took fractions of a second to shift from a dog to a flipping tree!

The tree rustled its branches - yes, it was moving like it had full control over every single leaf crowning its majestic limbs - and bent down a little as if to look at the two intruders.

"Gnomes got your tongue?" he asked in amusement when neither Macey nor Jared said anything. "I'm the Teacher, and I am indeed a kludde. Now, tell me, why have you entered our domain? The children said something about earthquakes?"

Macey looked up at the tree, wondering where exactly to look. It seemed impolite not to look the kludde in the eye when talking to him, but there were no eyes, nor a face in general. She ended up looking at the spot where the lowest branch left the main trunk.

"We spent some time with Jerimiah of the local kabouter clan," the kelpie began. "According to him, there have been earthquakes in the south, and when we left, there was a small one affecting his home too. But that's not the only reason we're here."

The tree shook its leaves, probably to show that he was still listening, so Macey continued, more confident this time.

"We've been travelling both on Earth and other planes and have fought two evil creatures bent on gaining power, no matter the consequences. One of them was feeding off the Staran, and we managed to destroy it. The other is still at large."

She quickly gave him a roundup of the Mahoun and what they knew about him. "We think the

Mahoun is planning to do something to the earth, or maybe already doing it. Those earthquakes could very well be part of his plan."

The tree gently moved from side to side as if he was deep in thought. "And why did you come here?"

This time, Jared responded. "The kabouters recommended we speak with you. Jerimiah said that the kludde have been behaving strangely recently, so we were wondering if you've felt the same evil approaching."

Suddenly, the bark of the tree began to glow and moments later, a man was standing in its place. His skin was like dark brown leather, thick and full of wrinkles, but his pale blue eyes looked surprisingly young. His hair was shaggy, hiding part of his face, yet even so, he had something imposing about him, and not just because he was two heads taller than Macey.

"Is this your real form?" she asked without thinking.

The man laughed. "What is your real form? Kelpie or human?"

She thought for a moment, then smiled. "Touche. I'm Macey and this is Jared."

"They call me Wilg when I'm not the Teacher," the kludde said in a grave voice, his laughter suddenly gone. "But I think I will need to be the Teacher for this." He sighed deeply. "Jerimiah is right. Something has been happening. At first, we thought nothing of it, then we thought it was a coincidence. For the past few weeks though, we've been more cautious - and now here you are, confirming our suspicions. In a way, I'm glad we now have a vague idea of what is the cause of the unrest."

Jared frowned and said what Macey was thinking. "What exactly has been happening?"

"Our young are having trouble shifting. Our old are getting weak and frail. The magic that connects us to the earth and sustains us is troubled, unpredictable. Even I, the chieftain of the kludde, am now feeling the effects."

"We are creatures of the earth. My tribe may live by the water, but in the end, we're bound to the earth. It gives us our unique abilities, the skill to change into whatever form we want. We're like clay that can be shaped into something new every time an artist touches it. Now, it's as if the earth has become too dry to take on new shapes without crumbling."

Macey shuddered at the thought of not being able to shift. It was a nightmare she'd had ever since she was a child, and it terrified her. She was both a human and a kelpie, and she would never want to have decide between one or the other.

"That must be terrible," she said, meaning every word. "Do you have any idea of what's causing it?"

The man shook his head. "I don't. We thought it was something in the ground that only affected us, but then a cousin from the earth kludde about a hundred kilometres from here sent word that they had the same problem. It's happening to all the kludde I know of."

"If it's the Mahoun, then there's not much we can do here," Jared sighed. "I doubt he's here physically; he's affecting too many areas at once. The earthquakes, the changes for the kludde, the strange energy I've felt when visiting the kabouters... It doesn't sound like it all has one single point of origin. He's attacking the earth in several ways at once, and the only way I can see us stopping this is confronting him directly."

"What I'm scared of is that this will never end," Macey said quietly. "Even if we defeat the Mahoun, there's so many more of these creatures out there. We don't know where they come from, we don't know how they spread, if they can breed and spread. Maybe all we're doing is blowing out individual candles when a giant wildfire is burning all around us."

Wilg looked at her sharply. "Did you say you killed one of them?"

Macey and Jared both nodded.

"Did one of you touch it?"

Again, Macey nodded. "I fought with it, before. It may have been in my head though, or maybe not, I'm not quite sure."

"Give me your hand."

What? Where was this going?

Gingerly, Macey stretched out her arm and the Teacher took her hand. His bark-like skin was rough but his grip was gentle.

"What are you doing?" Jared asked. She could feel the tension in him; he didn't like Wilg touching her. How was he fine with three other men being with her, but not with a kludde taking her hand? She was going to have a chat with him about that.

"Every death leaves a trace," the Teacher muttered, closing his eyes. Warmth spread through Macey's arm, an unnatural heat that was both uncomfortable and pleasant at the same time.

"The earth is like a library. Everything comes from her and everything ends up back in her arms. Every being has a connection to the earth, as faint as it may be. If I can isolate the trace, I will be able to search for its source."

That sounded complicated, and somehow, Macey doubted that Self-Doubt even had a physical form that could leave a residue on her. She was beginning to think that maybe those creatures weren't even from Earth. Maybe they were aliens? Spirits? Devils? Some kind of sentient magic?

Well, the important thing was that they needed to destroy them before they destroyed the world.

"You've been touched by something else," Wilg said suddenly.

"By several someones," Jared snickered quietly and Macey elbowed him until he quietened.

"It's a strange kind of energy. Something wild and untamed, yet it sits in you calmly."

Air. He had to mean Air.

"It's complicated," she hedged. "But it's not the enemy we're looking for."

The Teacher nodded. "I will move on then."

The heat on her skin increased and spread along her shoulder. What was the kludde doing to her?

She studied his face, which was much easier now that his eyes were closed. While Wilg's rough features were human, the smaller details weren't. His mouth was too wide, his nose too sharp. The wrinkles of his skin were thick and leathery, and looked so much like bark that she wanted to reach out and touch them. His bushy eyebrows almost connected in the middle, and the hair was so coarse that it reminded her of that of the elephant she'd once petted in a zoo.

The silence became uneasy as the two of them watched the kludde study her. Hopefully this wasn't all for nothing and he'd be able to tell her more about what was going on.

"Your future can take many different paths, none

of which have been defined yet," Wilg said, a glazed look coming into his eyes.

"Helpful," Jared muttered.

The kludde chuckled. "Maybe it is, maybe it isn't, but with so many souls tied to hers, it isn't surprising her future could go so many ways."

"You can tell the future?" Macey asked, a little in awe of the creature in front of her.

"Not as such," he admitted. "We can tell general information about the journey the traveller must take. It's why we're known for causing mischief. Often it isn't actually intended to take traveller's from their paths, but to put them back on the one they've strayed from."

"Ah," Jared said.

"And the multipath thing? Is that why the children seemed so..."

"Overexcited with you? Yes," Wilg confirmed. "It's rare we get travellers with more than one path at all. And even then they only have two, it confused them for a moment."

"So this really could go on forever." She didn't want to feel the defeat welling up inside her, but she also couldn't ignore it. How could she carry on when her entire life was going to be a series of battles she may or may not win.

"Or you could die," the kludde countered. "A

couple of the more visible paths suggested that could be your end."

"Everyone has to die," Macey said, her voice shaking with nerves. She didn't want to accept that she'd end up that way earlier than anticipated. She had a lot more living to do first. Maybe even a family of her own to start. Though she'd need to talk to her men about that. No way was she having a child with each of them. They were going to have to share whatever offspring came along. Then again, would Flint's fire even mix with her water?

"Yes, they'll mix fine," Wilg interrupted.

"What? How?"

"We're touching. I can't read your thoughts, but the paths coming from you change as you think. From the ones becoming the strongest, I can make a good guess at what you're thinking."

"Creepy," Jared muttered, giving Macey a conspiratorial grin first. "So what was she thinking?"

"About the best way to castrate incubi," the kludde said with a surprisingly straight face.

Macey muffled a giggle, not wanting to give the game away just yet. Jared's hands flew to his crotch, protecting his cock from the non-existent threat.

"What would happen if I chopped it off?" she asked him.

"You don't want to know." The tone his voice took was enough to warn her off the subject. Maybe she'd ask Cam when she returned to the others. It seemed like the kind of thing he'd know. Until then, she'd just have to help Jared avoid any cock threatening situations.

"Would it grow back?" she wondered, growing more intrigued by the second. As well as more amused, but that was mostly due to the bewildered look on Jared's face.

"I don't know, and I'm not going to cut it off to find out."

"Pity."

"Will you help us down the right path?" Jared asked the kludde, successfully steering conversation away from his genitals for probably the first time in his entire life.

"Yes, but to do so, I'll need you to trust me," Wilg said, his hand still clasped around Macey's. "Will you?"

"Yes." Her answer came without hesitation, which surprised her. She hadn't thought she'd trust strangers so easily, especially with Mahoun and the others existing with the sole intention of destruction.

ELEVEN

Macey shivered as she took in the weird stones surrounding them. At first, they'd seemed haphazardly placed, but the more she looked, the more logically they seemed to have been positioned. And they gave her an uneasy feeling.

"These are ancient," Jared observed.

"Very," the kludde responded. "It's said they're filled with magic from the very beginning of time, though there's no real evidence to support that. Even so, they have a magic no being I've ever met has the power of wielding. We're supposed to use them when someone needs guidance."

"Supposed?" Macey enquired.

"Well, not many people have ever known they could ask for it. And if they did, then they didn't do anything about it. Our kind has a bad reputation. Much like your own, I believe."

Macey nodded. It had been devastating to learn how the humans viewed kelpies. It was true that they weren't the most beautiful of creatures, but they were majestic in their own right. And they wouldn't hurt anyone. At least, not on purpose they wouldn't.

"What are we supposed to do?" she asked.

"He isn't supposed to do anything. He needs to stand outside the stones," Wilg said, nodding towards Jared.

"No way," the incubus responded. "I'm not leaving her to whatever weird ceremony you're going to perform."

"Jared," Macey cautioned.

"Please, this will only work if she's the only one within the stones with me. Or else your path will confuse matters."

"Path?" Macey asked. "He only has one?" She frowned, unsure what to make of that. Why would Jared only have the one path when she had many? As Wardens, surely they should have the same amount.

"Yes and no," the kludde replied. "He has many, but they are faint and following his main one, which is linked to you. Are you ready?"

Macey stared at the strange creature, confused by all that was going on. Despite that, she knew this could be a way in which she actually managed to progress on her quest to rid the world of Mahoun and his friends. Which always made things worth doing.

"Okay then. Jared, out of the circle."

"Macey..."

"Jared, now. I'm not spending my whole life chasing who knows what, to who knows where. I want answers and a direction that can take me where I really want to go. I want a life with you all, and we can't have that if we're always off saving the world."

He opened his mouth to speak but closed it again seconds later. With a confused look on his face and a reluctance which could rival that of the Pope's going into a brothel, he stepped away and to the other side of the surrounding stones.

"Good, we can begin," the kludde announced, rubbing his hands together with what appeared to be glee. Never a good sign if anyone asked Macey. It normally meant someone evil had worked on a plan and it was all coming together. At least in the films and books she'd encountered, the good guys still managed to save the day.

"What do you want me to do?" she asked, nerves tainting her question. She hated being so vulnerable, but knew it was a necessity.

"Just close your eyes and relax. Don't say anything else. You'll feel my presence within you, but remember I can't read your thoughts, only the paths you are able to take."

She nodded and did as he instructed. The world went black and she scrunched her hands into fists before releasing them again. This was uncomfortable to say the least. Hopefully they could be done with it quickly and she would be left to get on with whatever path he selected for her to walk.

The air thrummed with unfamiliar magic, both around the stones and around Macey herself. She wasn't actually sure where the kludde started and where the magic from the stones did. All she knew was that she didn't feel like her normal self.

Something tugged to the left and she turned, only to see a forest of flaming trees. Macey shrunk back, the heat almost burning her face before disappearing as the magic in the air shut it down. That wasn't the path she was supposed to take then. She couldn't say she wasn't relieved.

This time, the magic tugged her to the right, where a great wave crashed down onto a seaside town. Macey raised her hands and tried to ward it off, but her own magic was bound by that of the stones and nothing happened. Once again, the image was shut down. That path probably wasn't the right one to go down either.

The magic was back. This time it felt like it gripped around her whole body, turning her around so she was facing the opposite way to where she had before. Or at least, she thought so. There was no actual way for her to be sure. With her eyes closed and her other senses pretty much useless, she could have been standing completely still for all she knew.

As before, a scene rose up before her. An older version of herself sat in a comfy chair with a small bundle nestled in her arms. A door opened behind her and an older Flint stepped in, an adoring look on his face as he approached older-Macey and began to talk to her. Macey had no idea what they were saying, but the pure joy on their faces couldn't be denied. Older-Flint leaned down and tickled the bundle, which squirmed in older-Macey's arms. A baby. That was what it must be.

The scene faded away in front of her, this time much less abrupt than before. Somewhere deep inside, Macey knew this meant that path might still be possible, but it wasn't the one she should be taking now. A weird longing welled up inside her. She hadn't realised how much she wanted that until this very moment.

A new image drifted into being. It was Izban, his blue hair the only colour in the otherwise bleak and dark scene. He was talking to someone who purposely stayed in the shadows, his face hidden under a large black hood. Izban kept looking around, as if he was scared of being watched. Then he passed a little brown parcel to the hooded person and a flash of pain crossed his features. The metallic taste of betrayal ran over Macey's tongue. Somehow, she knew that's what Izban was doing. Betraying them.

Another scene started. Macey looked about the same as she did now, though she was surrounded by a whirlpool of water. Other-Macey lifted her hands up, controlling the water as it spun higher and higher into the sky.

A weird sensation made Macey step closer to the image, though the movement may well have been in her head rather than actually real. The vision changed, transforming before her into a great pit in the ground with Jared at the bottom and other Macey climbing down into it. The look on her face was pained but determined. Much like she'd actually feel if the situation arose.

The vision changed again, removing other-Macey and Jared from the equation completely as her other men rose to the forefront, the crashing waves of the sea behind them as it broke over the rocks.

They were in a small boat, shouting to one another and trying to gain control of it. Panic began to make itself known within her as she struggled to not to run to their aid. If they needed her help, then why were she and Jared still in Belgium with a kludde and not there? They shouldn't have split up in the first place.

As suddenly as it had all started, everything went

black and Macey swayed back and forth, her consciousness somewhere between awake and asleep.

Strong arms wrapped around her waist as the swaying intensified, almost going as far as falling.

"The sea," she muttered aloud. "We need to go to the sea."

"What?" a familiar voice asked.

"We need to go to the sea," she repeated, hoping Jared would listen this time. If it was Jared holding her at all. Though she was pretty sure it was.

"We can't go to the sea," he said.

"She's responding to what she saw in her visions," a different voice said. "It probably won't come to pass like she's seen it, but that's the path she needs to travel the most."

"And it'll end well?" Jared asked. His voice broke a little, betraying his concern over the whole thing. It would only have been noticeable to someone who knew him well and she longed to reach out and comfort him but didn't seem to have use of her arms yet.

"That will really depend on her."

"I can't travel on the Staran," Jared said, anguish spreading in his voice. "And I've used a lot of my earth magic to get us here. If I use any more, I won't be of any use once we get to the sea."

A sudden image appeared in Macey's mind, like an echo of the visions she'd been shown.

"I think I can do it," she muttered.

"But... only Cam and Flint are able to."

"That was before I helped heal the Staran," she said weakly, the last tendrils of the vision still running through her, making her unsteady on her feet. "I was inside of them, back when I first encountered Self-Doubt. I think it changed something. Let's try it, it's worth a stab."

Jared nodded. "Alright then. How do we do it?"

"I'll leave you to it," Wilg said with a smile. "It was a pleasure meeting you. May you always find the right path, and may you always find the way back."

Macey wasn't quite sure what to say to that, or if there was a phrase she was expected to say. "May the path be with you," she stuttered. "Thank you for your help."

"The kludde will be ready to assist you, should we be needed," the Teacher said while already turning away from them. "I hope you'll manage to heal the earth. The world. Everything. Your path will be difficult, but there is a chance that you may succeed."

With that ominous statement, he disappeared into the mists surrounding the stones.

"We will definitely succeed," Jared muttered defiantly. "There's no way we won't."

Macey gave him a grim smile. "We'll do our best. Now, any idea how to summon the Staran?"

Jared shrugged. "No idea. Maybe think of them?

Wish them into being? Honestly, I have no idea. Usually I travel with one of the others, and I've never thought to ask them how exactly they're doing it."

Oh well, Macey would just have to try. If her men could do it, so could she. At least, she hoped so. It was just a hunch after all, and all the earlier vision had shown her was them travelling on the Staran, not how she entered it. Maybe they'd supposed to ask Wilg for help? It was too late for that now.

She did as Jared had suggested and closed her eyes, thinking of the Staran.

"Tell me if anything happens," she warned the incubus, before focussing on the feeling of the Staran, the strange scent of them, the stomach-lurching feeling of travelling on them. She remembered the first time she'd done this. It felt so long ago, yet she could recall every detail. Every sensation.

She instinctively pushed her magic into that memory, and Jared whooped.

"It's there!" He hooked an arm around her waist. "Quick, think of where you want to travel and hopefully they'll get us there."

That's when Macey noticed that she had no idea of the actual place her men were. All she'd seen in the vision was the sea, with no visible land or islands in sight. But what was it what the guys had told her when they'd first taken her to travel on the Staran?

That they were sentient and sometimes knew where they were needed?

She brought the image back into her mind. Flint, Cam and Rónán in their little boat, the waves threatening to overturn it. The looks of panic on their faces.

Without thinking, she took a step forward – and was catapulted into the Staran.

Orca

TWELVE

"Ehm, Macey? How are you doing this?"

She opened her eyes and looked around. They were standing on solid ground – and below them was the sea. And the ground wasn't there. Their feet were on nothing but air. But it felt solid. Macey tentatively took a step forward. Yes, solid.

"I'm not doing anything," she said. "It must be the Staran."

"Well, they got us to the right place." Jared pointed to somewhere on the horizon. "I think I can see their boat. But now the big question is, how do we get down there? And then, how do we get to them? I'd like to avoid swimming in the ocean, if that's possible. I'm not a great swimmer."

"If it comes to that..." Macey took a deep breath. "I'd let you ride on me."

Jared stared at her, then broke into laughter. "I'd never thought I'd ever ride you in that way."

"I take it back. You'll have to swim."

Suddenly, a warm breeze surrounded them. It almost felt like a hug.

"Jared... I don't think the Staran are holding us up here."

His eyes widened slightly. "Air?"

Macey nodded. *Talia?* She asked in her mind, but didn't get a response. She hadn't really expected one. Air was living inside of her, but it was more like an extra source of magic rather than a person or spirit.

"Ehm, bring us down to them?" she asked tentatively. Luckily, Air seemed to understand. The warm breeze grew stronger and embraced them even tighter, until they began to move slowly, very slowly, through the nothingness of empty space above the sea.

"This is so weird," Jared muttered, and Macey wholeheartedly agreed. This way of travelling didn't rank very high in her list of transport methods. To be honest, most of her recent trips hadn't been very nice. Travelling through the earth with Jared... claustrophobic. Travelling on the Staran... creepy and nausea inducing. No, she much preferred swimming, walking, or even driving in a car. Maybe she was a bit conservative or anti-magic in that aspect.

The closer they got to the boat bobbing up and

down on the wild waves, the faster Macey's heart beat. The men in the boat seemed calm, not shouting like she'd seen in her vision. Did that mean they'd arrived after or before the events in the vision?

"They look okay," Jared said, echoing her thoughts. "Do you think they've dealt with the Orca yet?"

Macey shrugged. "No idea, but I think we're about to find out."

They were now within shouting distance, so Macey put two fingers in her mouth and whistled loudly. Her brothers had taught her to do that when she'd first come onto land.

The guys turned and even from the distance, Macey could see their jaws drop. They had to look ridiculous, floating down from the heavens like angels. Or demons, in Jared's case.

"Macey?" Cam shouted and Macey waved innocently.

"Hey guys! We didn't want to miss the party."

Inside, she wasn't feeling as calm as she pretended to be, but she didn't want to worry the men just yet. Maybe the battle was already over and everyone was safe. Maybe the vision of her standing inside that column of water wasn't going to happen, or some time in the future, not now.

Air pushed them forward one last time until they were hovering a few feet above the boat. Then she let them drop, and Macey landed in Flint's arms, his mouth pressing against hers before she could even react.

Jared hadn't landed as softly, judging from his shouts, but Macey didn't care. Flint's lips were teasing her, welcoming her, and all she could think about was how comfortable she felt in his arms. They'd not been separated for long, but a lot had happened since they'd split up at Malan's place.

"My turn," Cam grumbled and a moment later, Macey was ripped from Flint's arms. She opened her mouth to complain, but Cam used that opportunity to kiss her, his tongue meeting hers in a breathless kiss. He ran his hands over her back and she melted into his touch. Now that she was with all her men again, she could feel the pieces in her come together; pieces she hadn't even noticed breaking apart. Only now she felt how she'd not been whole.

But now she was.

When Cam ended the kiss, she stepped back and turned to Rónán. He was standing there, watching her, apparently not quite sure whether he could welcome her the same way as the other two.

She smiled at him and opened her arms. Faster than she could see, he'd moved to her and hugged her tight, his lips seeking hers.

"Sorry to interrupt your little boat trip, but have you fought the Orca yet?" Jared asked, reminding

Macey that they had more important things to do than kiss her men.

"Yes and no," Cam said, his demeanour turning serious. Macey broke the kiss and turned, leaning against Rónán who wrapped his hands around her waist.

"We found it, threw some magic at it, but it dived and disappeared without us being able to follow. So now we've been waiting here for it to resurface," Flint explained. "It's strong and seems quite resistant to magic. Even my fire didn't leave a trace on its skin. No idea why it fled and didn't fight."

"My fellow selkies are searching for it just now," Rónán said from behind her, his chest vibrating softly as he spoke. "They don't have a chance fighting it, but they'll try and drive it to the surface so we can attack it. They're giving me updates every few minutes." He sighed. "It's attacked two of their settlements already and several selkies have died. We need to kill it as soon as possible before it can slay any more of my people."

"Why can't the selkies fight it?" Macey asked in confusion. "Don't you have magic?"

"Most of us don't," Rónán explained sadly. "I'm a bit of an anomaly. I know most kelpies have magic; maybe that's why my people are jealous of you. The intrinsic selkie magic allows us to shift, but having offensive magic like me is rare."

Macey almost felt sorry for the selkies. It was natural to her to have magic; and she couldn't imagine having shifting as her only power. Sure, it was great to be able to be both a kelpie and human, but she loved her water magic and the thrill it gave her whenever she used it.

"So all we can do is wait?" she asked at the same time as a seal head broke the surface. She stared at it in wonder. It was larger than a normal seal, and the skin seemed to glitter in a slightly blue hue. She'd never seen a shifted selkie before; especially since Rónán wasn't able to shift for some reason.

The selkie made a strange noise and Rónán moved to the edge of the boat to talk to it with the same whining sounds. It was a very different language to the clicks the kelpies used to communicate.

"It's about a mile away," Rónán translated and pointed to their left. "That way. It's getting closer to the surface, so we might have a chance this time."

The boat began to move and it took Macey a second to realise that it was Cam propelling it with his wind.

The selkie dived and disappeared in the dark waters.

"Was that a friend of yours?" she asked Rónán and he grimaced.

"I wouldn't call her a friend exactly. More like a

bully who I'd usually avoid. But right now, we're all working together to fight the Orca."

The boat was racing over the waves, sea foam flying through the air and hitting Macey's face. She wiped it away, tasting the salt as it touched her lips. She preferred freshwater, but swimming in the wild sea was almost as good. They didn't have many waves in the loch she'd grown up in, only during the winter storms.

"Almost there," Cam warned them. "Better prepare for a fight."

They spread out so that they were able to watch the water around them in all directions. There was no sign of the Orca, nor of any selkies.

"Did you manage to injure it at all?" she asked.

"I don't think so," Flint replied, frustration lacing his voice. "But it dived too quickly so we didn't get to check. Let's hope we can engage it longer this time."

The vision of the whirlpool flashed through Macey's mind. Maybe that was the answer. If she managed to create a 'hole' in the water so the Orca couldn't escape, the others might be able to kill it. But would she be strong enough? Her powers had increased, but creating a whirlpool like in the vision seemed way too difficult. If she failed, she might sink the boat.

Another selkie head broke the surface and said something to Rónán.

"It's coming," he warned the others. "Prepare yourselves, it's almost below us."

Macey looked around, hoping to spot the Orca before it reached the boat. A dark shadow appeared to her right, far bigger than she'd expected.

"Holy waves," she muttered, before raising the alarm. "Over here!"

The others turned to face the shadow that was rising quickly to the surface. It was too fast, too big. It was going to hit the boat.

"Brace yourselves!" Macey shouted and clutched the railing just in time. The Orca's head crashed into the boat's side and the sound of splintering wood filled the air. There were screams behind her, but she didn't have time to turn around before she was thrown into the sea, the piece of railing she was still holding flying along with her.

She broke the water's surface and before she could react, the shift came over her. She had no choice in the matter; one moment she was human, the next kelpie. She'd never shifted this quickly before. It should have scared her, but there wasn't time. Her men were in danger.

She focussed on finding them. Not many people knew that the antenna on her head was her seventh sense, a way to locate warm bodies in the water. Maybe it had evolved as a way to find other kelpies in large bodies of water, or prey – it didn't matter.

She sensed all four of them, three of them struggling in the water, one swimming confidently. That had to be Rónán. He didn't need any help, so she focused on the other three.

Two of them were close together, but the other one was drifting off, sinking further with every untrained swim stroke. Her antenna sense couldn't tell her who it was, but he needed help, no doubt about that.

She swam to him as fast as she could, but before she could reach him, her senses alerted her to another presence. Something big was approaching her from behind.

The Orca.

She turned and stared right into its open maw, rows of sharp teeth waiting to rip her apart. It was massive, far bigger than even a blue whale, and its eyes were glinting red with cruelty and hunger.

This was not a being that could be bargained with.

She hissed and turned, swimming away from it as fast as she could, hoping she could draw it away from her men. She hissed sharply while swimming, the kelpie version of a war cry.

The Orca was much faster than her though, no matter how quickly she swam. She pushed some magic into the water around her, propelling her through the water. Now she was able to match the

Orca's speed, but she knew that she was using up a lot of power this way. She needed to confront him soon, before her energy ran out. But how was she supposed to fight this monster on her own?

The image of the whirlpool flashed through her mind again. There had to be a reason why she'd been shown that vision. Maybe she should just try to create something like it. But once she did, she wouldn't have the energy to fight it. She needed her guys.

Macey changed direction again, swimming back to where the boat had been destroyed. She pushed herself to swim even faster, to get some distance between herself and the Orca.

When she got closer, her antenna sense told her that there were other people swimming with her men. Each of them was held by at least two selkies who were helping them stay afloat. She'd never thought that she'd ever be indebted to a selkie, but right now, she was prepared to hug and kiss them all and promise them half her loch kingdom. Not that it was hers to give away, but it was the thought that counted.

If only she could communicate with them to tell them what she was planning. She'd told Jared of her vision though, so hopefully he'd be able to figure it out.

Once she'd reached a safe distance, she stopped.

In the vision, she'd had been human, not kelpie, but there was no time to shift, and her water magic was a little stronger in her kelpie form anyway.

She took a deep breath, her gills filtering the oxygen out of the cold ocean water.

The Orca was almost upon her again. Time to weave some magic.

She whinnied and expelled her magic, letting it form a small tornado that gripped the water and carried it with it, condensing it, then lifting it into the air as if she was trying to empty out the sea. Slowly, a funnel began to form like a spear of air penetrating the water.

Her body shook with effort, but she kept pouring her magic into the whirlpool that was roaring before her. The Orca was fighting against the current, struggling not to be pushed into the hole in the ocean that Macey had created.

It wasn't strong enough. One moment, only its head was poking into the air, then the whole body was in the centre of the column of water, held there by... by what, exactly? Was it Air or perhaps Cam's wind magic? She didn't have the strength to look and see, but all that mattered was that the Orca was out of the water and in reach.

A ball of fire shot through the air and landed on the Orca's black skin, but it dissipated as soon as it touched the skin. There was no mark on the Orca, no trace of a wound. Flint threw more fire at the whale; balls, lances, rains of sparks. None of it seemed to injure the Orca.

Sweat was forming on Macey's scales, carried away by the water. She wasn't going to be able to keep this up much longer.

Then, a spear flew from the water, landing on the Orca's flank. It fell into the depths of the whirlpool, not leaving a scratch on the whale's skin, but more spears followed, thrown by selkies suddenly surrounding Macey.

While they didn't harm the whale, they certainly enraged it, and it flung its tail up and down, struggling against the hold the air had on it. More fire rained down on it, setting some of the spears alight. The first fiery spear embedded itself in the Orca's back. It wasn't deep, but it was more than they'd managed before.

The selkies and Flint seemed to coordinate their attacks, with the wraith setting the spears on fire just before they hit the whale.

Suddenly, a bolt of lightning shot through the air, blinding Macey momentarily. Amber!

She looked up through the murky sea, just about to make out the beithir flying above the wide opening of the whirlpool. Someone was sitting on her back, presumably Izban.

Icicles rained from the sky; the mage's doing. And

just when Macey thought that everybody was fighting the Orca, a spear-shaped lance of pressed together sand rose from the depths, embedding itself in the Orca's soft belly.

It roared in pain, writhing in fury.

Black dots were dancing before Macey's eyes. Her magic was about to run out, but it wasn't enough yet. She needed to keep up the whirlpool. The Orca wasn't defeated yet; they needed more time.

Breathing became difficult, but she didn't stop pouring every single drop of magic into the column.

Her vision faded, the spots turning into a dark screen. Her mind became foggy and with a final breath, she expelled her last bit of magic, before letting herself drift off into the blackness.

Something pushed her back just before she lost consciousness; a shockwave of sort. She smiled. Hopefully, the Orca had been defeated.

THIRTEEN

"Macey," Jared called, shaking her gently as she roused from sleep. Or exhaustion. Realistically, that option did seem more likely.

"Mmm?" Maybe if she didn't move much, he'd get into bed with her. Or one of the others would. If they wrapped her up in their arms, then rest would be all the sweeter. There was something about the comfort only her men could bring.

"We need you to wake up," he said. "We need to move, but can't until you're awake."

"Mm-what?" she murmured, but opened her eyes all the same. Not that it helped. They were still sticky from sleep and refusing to focus properly.

"We're by the side of the ocean and we need you to wake up so you can finish shifting," Cam said, his words surprisingly calm given the situation she'd found them in.

"Oh," she muttered, glancing down at herself and discovering she was still partially shifted. Luckily for her, the lower half of her body was still submerged in water, so she hadn't dried out.

With a single thought, she shifted completely back to human, leaving her naked and shivering with exertion.

"What happened?" she asked, looking up at the men surrounding her. Each of them wore a concerned expression. Except for Rónán, who wasn't even looking at her, but over her shoulder with a disgusted grimace tugging at his lips.

"We defeated it," he said, lifting his hand and pointing in the direction he was staring.

Macey shuffled in her spot on the floor to try and work out what he was getting at, before gagging slightly.

The Orca was dead alright. But it didn't look anything like she expected a dead orca to. Instead, it's inky black skin was leaking off it's body and pooling into the sea. It reminded Macey a little of the oil slicks she'd seen on TV during her stay on earth. Even just the images left her feeling sticky and slimy in a way she hadn't expected. It was like she felt the oil itself throughout her whole body. And this time wasn't any different. She could sense the sea crying out to her, even as it took away the odd substance.

"Why is it doing that?" she whispered.

"I'm not sure," Rónán answered. "I suspect its evil is being reabsorbed by the sea."

"But that's not a good thing, is it?" She hated just how unsure she sounded, but had to admit the whole conversation was a little bit weird. Then again, most of the conversations she had with her men could be deemed a little weird. Unless it was about waffles. That wasn't weird in the slightest. Everyone in the world should have regular conversations about waffles. It just made sense.

"Yes and no," Rónán replied. "For the immediate area, probably not. But in the grand scheme of things...this evil is just like the food chain. Orcas are at the top, plankton are at the bottom." He shrugged as if that were all there was to it.

"But if orcas are at the top anyway, then why did we bother defeating this one?" It all made no sense to her.

"This one wasn't a real orca," Flint pointed out. "Any real animal would have at least been injured by my flames the first time."

"Oh." It took a moment to process in Macey's head. "But how did we defeat it?" She frowned, trying to recall the events, but it was all a mess of rushing water and panic in her mind.

"You held it steady in a whirlpool and I managed to flame it. With the help of the selkies. Amber and Izban, of course." Flint nodded his head to Rónán, a sign of respect if ever she saw one.

Macey nodded. Anything which had her men playing nicely was good in her book.

"So, what do we do now?" she asked.

"Rónán is going to take us back to the selkie settlement," Cam said. "We can rest safely there and work out what our best move is."

"Is that a good idea?" Macey looked at Rónán, the worry she was feeling coming through in her eyes and begging him to answer her unspoken questions.

"You just helped them defeat the biggest threat they've ever faced. I doubt it matters to most of them that you're a kelpie." He gave her an easy smile in reassurance. It almost worked. There was only a small part of her doubting whether or not this was a good idea. Probably not, but what choice did she have? It wasn't like they were close to a hotel or anything. The isles around St. Kilda weren't exactly known for their habitability.

"Hmm."

"You'll be fine." Rónán took a step forward and slipped an arm around Macey's waist, crushing her to him. He kissed her softly on the cheek and gave her another reassuring grin. "It'll be fine, Macey," he repeated.

"I hope you're right," she responded.

"Shall we?" Jared interrupted. "I'm hungry."

"We didn't have dinner that long ago," Macey chided.

"We didn't get any waffles though, did we?"

"You went all the way to Belgium and didn't get any waffles?" Flint demanded, his eyes widening with shock.

"We were rudely interrupted by an earthquake," Macey mumbled. The world really had it out for her. Every time she got close to eating some delicious waffley goodness, fate cruelly snatched that chance away.

"An acceptable excuse," Cam acknowledged.

"Shouldn't we wait for Amber and Izban?" Macey asked, trying to distract herself from the waffle loss and failing miserable.

Rónán shook his head. "No need, Cara has shown them the way."

Despite the slightly distasteful way he said the other woman's name, a spike of jealousy flared into life within her. She didn't like the idea of another woman talking to her man. Not when it was clear they shared some kind of history.

"Cara?"

"The selkie I talked with earlier," he supplied.

Macey scowled. She really didn't like the sound of the other woman. He'd said she was a bully, but that wasn't necessarily the whole truth. There was always something more when the male kelpies said things about that to the female ones.

"Right."

"Shall we?" Rónán asked, apparently oblivious to the way Macey was feeling. She nodded despite herself. It was better to get this over with than to draw it out any longer than necessary. Plus, all she was going to do was torture herself with thoughts of Cara anyway. Until she saw her in human form at least.

Selkie

A large bonfire crackled in the space between several mud huts, the heat reaching Macey's face and warming her entire body. She didn't really feel the cold, but it's presence was somewhat soothing and filled her with a comforting feeling she couldn't quite put her finger on.

Flint stared into the flames but didn't step any further. He was probably worrying about abusing the selkies' hospitality or something along those lines. It was hard to tell with the fire wraith.

"Make yourselves at home," Rónán announced, waving a hand around the settlement.

"Macey!" Amber called, waving frantically from a place across the fire. She was draped in what appeared to be some kind of animal hide, definitely not her usual kind of outfit. She must have flown here without stopping to pack first.

The redhead started rushing over to the other Wardens, her blue-haired mage trailing behind her and looking as miserable as ever. Macey was determined to get a smile off him one day. It seemed impossible, but she'd just have to keep trying.

"Hey," she said, embracing the other woman once she'd reached them. "How did you get here?"

"I flew," Amber pointed out.

"Oh, sorry. I meant, how did you know to get here," Macey corrected herself. The flying thing should have been obvious given Amber's unusual dress and the fact she'd seen her in beithir form anyway.

"Malan sent word you'd need us," the redhead replied, shrugging. "I swear, if these prophets know so much, why don't they just tell us it straight in the first place?"

Macey scoffed. Amber did have a point. Though the answer was probably something like it not working if they knew all the answers. If Macey never had to deal with another prophet in her life, she'd be one happy kelpie.

"They probably think we don't have anything better to do than chase around vague hints," she said.

This time, it was Amber who laughed. "Or maybe

they're just trying to make sure you don't spend all your time in bed with your men. Not that anyone would blame you." She winked at the same time Izban scowled, clearly not impressed by his girlfriend's reaction.

Macey said nothing, but that didn't stop her ears heating in embarrassment. She really wished they'd stop doing that. It was somewhat cliched.

"Have you met Cara yet?" Amber asked, changing tack.

"No," Macey replied, trying to push down the jealousy she was feeling once more. Maybe she was more like Izban that she thought. If so, maybe they could bond over the annoying feelings inside them.

"Come with me." Amber grabbed her hand and pulled her off in the direction she'd come from. "I'll be right back," she called over her shoulder to Izban, who was left looking a little lost until Flint walked up to him and started chatting.

Macey stumbled over a loose stone in the ground. That's what she got for watching her men and not where she was putting her feet.

They reached the other side of the fire in a matter of moments and Macey gulped loudly. There was only one woman who wasn't busy in conversation and she was intimidating to say the least. She had long blonde hair and the biggest blue eyes Macey had ever seen. They sparkled in the fire light, whether from the flicker of the flames themselves, or from the magic within the selkies, Macey didn't know, but the effect was dazzling and beautiful beyond words.

"This is Cara," Amber introduced. "My friend, Macey. I was telling you about her."

Macey smiled at the stunning woman, hoping she wasn't coming across as insecure as she felt.

"Hi." She held out her hand and waited for the selkie to take it.

"So you're the kelpie that has Rónán all tied up in knots," Cara sneered instead of responding to the introduction.

Concern flickered over Amber's face as she realised the introduction wasn't going to plan. Macey reached out and gave the beithir's hand a reassuring squeeze. None of this was her fault after all. She'd just been trying to do the polite thing.

"I wouldn't say tied up in knots," Macey replied sweetly. "I think he's perfectly in control of his emotions."

"Unlikely when he's been bewitched."

The way Cara said the final word had Macey recalling what Rónán had said earlier. If not all selkies had magic, then she suspected Cara was one of those. And that would mean her problem with Macey was that she could do magic and not anything else. She sighed with relief. If that was the problem, she could deal with it. What she didn't want to deal with was a jealous selkie out to get her.

"My magic is tied to the water." Well, and air. "Not anything like emotions, love or that kind of thing." Macey kept her voice light, not wanting to give anything away. She was definitely getting better at keeping her feelings in check. She had the Voice's imprisonment to thank for that one.

"Love?" Cara raised a disdaining eyebrow. "You dare use that word?"

"Why wouldn't I?" Macey asked. "If that's how we feel." She knew she was treading on thin ice, but felt a little too much joy at the selkies discomfort to stop. This was far too much fun.

"You can't possibly know what love is you vi... Rónán!" Cara's voice and disposition changed in an instant, causing jealousy to surge again within Macey.

A warm hand landed on the small of her back and she relaxed into Rónán's touch, pleased he was here reaffirming what she already knew about their relationship.

"Hello, Cara." His voice was cool and collected. It wasn't likely that these two were friends then. That was always a good sign.

"How have you been?" she purred, pushing past Macey and stepping between her and Rónán.

Oh, that wasn't good. Not at all.

"Tired, but it's been a long day. I thought I'd come and ask if Macey's ready for bed." Rónán's corresponding smile was faker than any Macey had given the other selkie, which gave her a great sense of contentment. He wasn't into this in the slightest.

"Great idea," she said, but didn't try to move the selkie draped all over him out of the way.

"Good night, Cara," Rónán said, dipping his shoulder and letting her touch fall from him.

"Good night," Macey added sweetly before slipping her arm around Rónán's waist.

"Ready?" he asked her. She nodded once.

"Night, Amber," Macey called.

"Night," the beithir answered, already only half paying attention as she looked around for her mage. Macey smiled to herself. She was grateful her friend had someone of her own to take care of and take care of her. Despite Izban's somewhat sour disposition, he was good to Amber.

"So...Cara?" Macey prodded once they were out of earshot.

Rónán sighed. "Where to even start with her," he muttered. "She's one of the leaders' daughters."

"One of?"

"Yes, he has six. She's the youngest and the most spoiled. Though the others are almost as bad. You'd have thought he'd have stopped after the first one."

Macey laughed. "Not a fan of the family?"

"Not at all. They look down on just about any selkie who is born beneath them. Which is pretty much all of us."

"So why was she draping herself all over you like a monkey in a banana tree?"

Rónán gave her a confused look. "A monkey?"

"You know, clinging to you as if you were the last selkie alive and you were her only chance to repopulate the earth with seal shifters."

Rónán stared at her, slightly shocked. "You realise seal shifters and selkies are two very different species, right?"

"They are? Huh." She hadn't given it much thought, if she was honest. She'd never really had to. "Okay, sorry. Repopulate with selkies then."

Rónán's next sigh was when Macey realised he was just trying to avoid her question, so she waited for him to go on. "Because to her, that's what I am. Not all selkies have magic like me, but that didn't used to be the case. Hundreds of years ago, all selkies had magic. But our bloodlines have become somewhat tainted over the years..."

"By humans?" Macey interrupted.

"Yes, by humans. And other races, I suspect, but I have no real proof of those. Anyway, our bloodlines became polluted and now there's less of us born with the ability to actually use magic. Everyone else is just stuck with the shifting side of things, and even that isn't quite like yours."

"Not like mine how?" she prompted, but he ignored her.

"Cara decided years ago that the best solution to her lack of magic was to mate with me and have children. I doubt she could gain power directly with that plan, but I think she'd be able to make a good grab for it in her children's names." He shrugged.

"This is about power?" Macey's jaw dropped open, not wanting to believe what she was hearing.

"Isn't everything? Isn't what Mahoun and the others are doing just the same?"

"I suppose so." She frowned. She'd never really thought about it like that. Or maybe she had and just couldn't remember. "Sorry, I'm tired. My brain is a little slow right now."

"We're almost home," he reassured her, his arms supporting her shoulders.

"Home?"

"My house. It's not very big, but the bed is large enough for the two of us. Three, even, if one of the others wants to join us, but you look like all you want is sleep."

Macey nodded. "Yeah, I'd like to be horizontal now."

The house turned out to be a thatched little hut with a high roof that made it look a bit like a tent. Rónán really hadn't lied when he'd said that it wasn't big.

"Where are the others going to sleep?" Macey muttered as Rónán unlocked the door for them.

"Several selkies have offered their hospitality. You saved them, so they'll look after them, don't worry."

"Good." She nodded and let Rónán push her forwards into the house. It was one big room that was separated into smaller areas by wooden screens. Everything had a rather rustic look, and not a single wall was straight.

"Driftwood," Rónán explained before she could even ask. "No trees here, so we take what we can from the ocean. The roof is partly thatched with kelp."

"Bed?"

He chuckled. "Behind the screen on your left."

Compared to the rest of the hut, the bed was rather large. Macey sat on the edge and let herself fall backwards, half asleep already.

She muttered thanks when Rónán began to take off her shoes, but she was fast asleep before he'd managed to undress her.

FIFTEEN

"Do you have it back?"

"Not yet, mother. I'm working on it."

"You shouldn't be here without it. It's a disgrace."

Slowly, Macey woke to the sound of voices. The sun was warming her face, and judging from its position, it had to be at least late morning.

"You'll never find a girl without your skin," the unfamiliar woman said in the distance. Her voice was shrill and unpleasant, and Macey was tempted to throw some water magic at her to shut her up.

"I've found one already, mother, and she-"

"A kelpie." The woman's voice quivered with disgust. "Of course one of those would accept a selkie man without his skin. No standards, those kelpies. They probably whore around with anyone."

"Mother!" Rónán admonished her loudly. "She

saved us all. She killed the Orca. You'd likely not even be here if she hadn't come to help, so please, just keep your opinions to yourself."

The woman muttered something Macey couldn't understand, but apparently, Rónán had heard it.

"Out," he said harshly. "And never say that again in my presence."

"I'm ashamed of you, son."

"Well, that's mutual," Rónán seethed. "Now go before Macey wakes up."

The door slammed shut and Macey decided it was time to stop pretending to be asleep.

"What the waves was that about?" she asked with a yawn. Rónán turned around to her and was by her side in a flash.

"Feeling better?"

Macey nodded. "Aye, I'm a lot less tired. Is your mother always this... ehm..."

"Spiteful?" He sighed and sat down on the bed. "Yes, she is. She's become a lot worse since my father left her. It's one of the reasons I don't spend much time here. I can't deal with her accusations and prejudice."

"We can't choose our parents." Macey put a hand on Rónán's arm. "You've turned out remarkably well though."

He chuckled deeply. "I take after my dad. He's very different from her. No idea how they ever got together, but I'm glad he left. She terrorised him, belittled him no matter what he did. He's a lot happier now that they're separated."

"Does he live in this settlement too?"

"No, he's moved away. He's... how shall I say this... He's turned his back on the selkie ways and is now living with a human woman. Usually it's selkie women who leave us and live with human men, but occasionally, it happens to selkie men too. I think my father's happy though. His new wife is lovely, even though she tries to ignore all existence of the supernatural. She likes to find excuses for things she can't explain."

Macey laughed. "I wonder what she'd say if she saw me shift."

Rónán joined her laugh. "She'd probably faint. Or go to a therapist because she'd think that she was experiencing hallucinations. She's a bit strange, but nice."

Macey tried not to think of her own strange family situation. Her mother who maybe wasn't her mother at all, and her aunt who may be her mother. It was confusing. She really needed to seek out Nessie soon to find out what the truth was.

To distract herself, she asked, "What did your mother mean at the beginning? About you not having your skin?"

Rónán sighed. "Our shifting magic is different from yours. When we shift from selkie to human, we step out of our seal skin. It isn't as gross as it sounds, by the way. Once we're fully human, the skin shrinks until it's small enough to be worn as a pendant. Some wear it on their belts, some as a necklace. Without it, we can't shift back to selkie."

Macey's eyes widened. "And you don't have your skin anymore?"

His shoulders drooped. "It was stolen about a year ago. They attacked me in the dark of night and ripped my necklace off. I still don't know who did it, but I assume it was other selkies. I'm not the most popular person here because I don't always want to stick to our traditional ways. I tried to find it, or find out who took it, but I've not had any success. Luckily, I have enough magic to dive underwater for almost as long as I could in selkie form, so it's not inhibited me as much as they probably hoped. Still, it's like a part of me is missing."

That, Macey could understand. If she couldn't shift... waves, she'd go crazy.

"Izban," she suddenly said, speaking at the same time as having the idea. "He can do spells to find things. He had a tracking spell once that he used to follow Amber when she was kidnapped."

Rónán frowned. "He doesn't seem to like me much. Do you think he'd do that for me?"

Macey laughed. "I don't think Izban likes anyone

besides himself and Amber. But I know exactly how to bribe him."

IZBAN AND AMBER were sitting outside a hut that looked exactly like Rónán's, snuggled against each other. They looked very cute together and Macey hated to disturb them, but Rónán needed the mage's help. She couldn't believe that the selkie hadn't been able to shift for a year now. She'd probably be dead by now, but he didn't seem to be affected at all. Yet another difference between the selkies and kelpies.

"Good morning," she greeted them and Amber flashed her a wide smile. "I never got to thank you two for coming to help."

In a way, she had talked to Amber about it, but not to Izban, and he was the one she was trying to charm.

"We wouldn't have been able to defeat the Orca without you. Especially you, Izban."

Okay, maybe that was a little bit over the top. Izban seemed to have noticed that too, for he started to scowl.

"What do you want?"

Amber elbowed her boyfriend. "Be polite," she hissed and he had the decency to look a little guilty.

"Good morning," he corrected himself, the scowl still on his face though. "What brings you here?"

Amber elbowed him again and he winced. "What? I said good morning!"

"It's the way you said it," the beithir explained patiently, sounding as if she'd had that conversation many times before. "You need to be polite to others and then they'll be polite to you."

Macey tried to hide a grin. Those two were behaving like an old couple.

Izban sighed. "Good morning, it's lovely to see you. Please, sit down."

Amber laughed. "See, much better."

Rónán and Macey sat down on a wobbly bench beside them.

"How did you sleep?" the selkie asked, playing along with the small talk game.

"Lovely, thank you." Amber smiled cheekily. "The bed was very soft."

Izban winced again, this time from embarrassment. "It was," he muttered. "Is it okay now to ask why they're here?"

"I need your help," Rónán said before Macey could prolong the awkward conversation any further. "I've been told you can find things with your magic. Something of mine was stolen and I need it back."

"Can't you just go to the selkie police or whatever you people have?"

"We don't have a police," Rónán explained patiently. "We have a Council of Elders who would judge and punish the culprits, but I don't know who actually stole it, so they're not much use to me."

"I'm sure Izban is going to..." Amber began, but her boyfriend cut her off.

"Tracking spells are difficult and time-consuming. You'll need to find yourself another mage."

That's what Macey had feared, but luckily, she had a secret weapon. One she'd hoped she wouldn't have to use. She leaned over to Izban and whispered, "In the visions I was shown by the kludde, I saw you betray us. Maybe it's a future that'll never happen, maybe you'll stay loyal, but if you don't help Rónán, I will tell Amber."

She retreated, feeling increasingly guilty at how she was blackmailing the mage. He stared at her, his eyes full of emotion that she couldn't interpret. Was he angry at her? Would he snap?

She still hadn't figured Izban out. He was so nice and gentle with Amber, but to the rest of them, he was cold and rude. He was an enigma that she really wanted to solve... some day. Right now, there wasn't time, so had to resort to cruder methods, like blackmail.

The mage met her eyes and she held his gaze. He was probably trying to see if she was bluffing. Well, she wasn't. This was about one of her men's happiness, and maybe even health, so she'd do whatever it took to set things right.

After what seemed like an eternity, he turned, breaking eye contact.

"Alright. Tell me what's missing."

Macey let Rónán do the explaining. Amber gasped when the selkie told them how he hadn't been able to shift in almost a year. As a shifter herself, she had to find that as terrible to imagine as Macey did.

"You need to help him," the beithir said as soon as Rónán had finished. "He's done so much for us, now it's our turn."

Izban stared into space for a moment, before turning to the selkie. "I need some of your hair."

Without hesitation, Rónán ripped out a few hairs and handed them to the mage. "Anything else? If I need to give you some of my fingernails for you to find my skin, I'll do that too."

Izban cringed. "No thanks, I don't need any other body parts. The hair will suffice."

Selkie Woman

"Are you sure this is going to work?" Rónán whispered to Macey as they watched Izban.

The mage had been in what appeared to be a trance like state and ignoring the rest of them.

"I don't really know. I haven't known him anywhere near long enough to be able to tell when things are going well or not." She shrugged, hoping to drive the point home. She could ask Amber, but the beithir was sat staring dreamily at her mage as if he could do no wrong.

Macey knew differently. His betrayal was coming and she had to make sure it had as little impact as possible. There was a chance it wasn't even going to come to pass. If what the kludde had said about the different paths was true. Even the one that had come true hadn't exactly passed like the vision suggested it would.

"Are you okay?" Rónán asked.

"Yes," she answered a little too quickly.

He raised an eyebrow. "You can talk to me, anytime you want. I know you haven't known me as long as the others, but…"

"But nothing," she protested. "You're as important to me as they are, even if I've known you for less time." She believed every word too. Before coming to land, she'd hardly believed in love, never mind true love. And even when she had spent some time on land, she'd still thought it was some odd notion humans had taken to in their stories and fables. But she wasn't so sure anymore. She knew how her men made her feel. And how much she wanted to be around them. None of them were more important than the others. It just didn't work like that.

"Then talk to me," he prompted.

Macey glanced at Izban, making sure he was still in his trance. "In Belgium, Jared and I met a kludde." She looked at him impatiently until he nodded to let her know he knew what that was. "One of the visions I had was of Izban betraying us."

"Ah, I see."

"You do?"

"Yes. You saw a vision and became convinced it would come to pass, even though it might not."

"Pretty much."

"I've fallen for that one myself. While I was travelling in Ireland, I came across a battlefield. I can't even remember who was fighting, probably some faeries of some kind. That lot are always at each other's throats." He waved his hand in dismissal, as if accepting what he was saying wasn't all that important. "Before the battle came, a crow circled overhead and cried out a prophecy about a death. Of one of the leaders no doubt. Knowing how it would turn out, the faerie on that side changed tactics and the person in question survived."

"A crow?" she mused. It seemed unlikely it was just a crow. If it was speaking and prophesying, then maybe it was more like Luch had been. Though the mouse shifter had been the first ever Warden and it seemed unlikely that there'd been two of them.

"Yes. I know it seems silly to think it was just a crow given the true state of the world, but..."

"No, I believe you. It could easily have been a talking crow." The words should have sounded mocking but actually didn't. Such was the advantage of having supernatural boyfriends. It wasn't like they'd misinterpret something she said and take offense.

"Exactly. But you shouldn't put too much stock in visions and prophecies. Have you ever heard of the butterfly effect?"

Macey shook her head, wondering what butterflies had to do with anything. As far as she could tell, they served no real purpose other than to look pretty and spread pollen about.

"It suggests that even something as small as the beat of a butterfly's wings is enough to change the future."

"Ah." She thought for a moment. "So by using Izban's betrayal against him now, I've probably changed how things will play out."

"It seems likely. If he knows you're watching his every move, it'll mean he either doesn't do it, or finds even sneakier ways to go about what he's going to do."

"I'm not sure which of those is the better option," Macey replied.

"I guess that's all going to depend on why he was going to betray you," Rónán pointed out. "Maybe he has good reason to do it. Or maybe it's Amber's life on the line. Can you honestly say you wouldn't betray someone to save one of us? Or that we wouldn't to save you?"

As much as she wanted to deny it, she knew she probably couldn't. There was too much between them. She'd do anything for them, even if it meant hurting someone else in the process. An uneasy feeling settled over her. That wasn't a pleasant thing to admit to anyone.

Luckily, Izban chose that moment to awaken from the trance and stare at them wide-eyed.

"I know where it is. And who stole it, although I can't remember her name."

"Her name? It was a woman?" Rónán stared at the mage. "Are you sure?"

Izban frowned. "Are you doubting my magic?"

"No, it's just that I assumed it would have been one of the men who are also in line to be clan chief. A selkie without his skin can't become chief, so it would have made sense for them to disable me like that."

The mage nodded grudgingly. "Yes, that makes sense, but I assure you, it was a woman. I saw her last night by the fire, but I have no idea what she's called. Amber spoke to her though, and Macey."

"Cara," both women said at once. Anger bubbled up in Macey's throat. She was going to kill that selkie for putting her man through all that.

"Bitch," she exclaimed, earning herself a raised eyebrow from Rónán.

"Why would she do such a thing?" he asked in confusion.

Amber looked at Macey, rolling her eyes.

"Men..." the beithir muttered, before explaining, "She clearly wants you for herself. She probably thought that taking away your skin would make you stay here, with her, and stop you from leaving."

"But why didn't she give it back when she noticed that it didn't work?"

Macey huffed. "Jealous women can be patient. She was probably hoping that you'd change your mind soon, once being without your skin got unbearable. Maybe she would have started blackmailing you soon."

She shot an apologetic glance at Izban, who ignored it. Maybe telling him about the vision had been foolish and rash. She just hoped that she hadn't set some things in motion that would end up hurting her or her men. Or the world, in the worst case scenario.

"Would you like us to come with you?" she asked the selkie, but he shook his head, his expression grim.

"No, I'm going to settle this myself. I'll show you were the others stay, and then I'll confront Cara."

Amber and Izban seemed happy to stay on their little bench, so Macey simply gave them a wave and followed Rónán through the village.

They stopped in front of one of the largest huts.

"The guest house," Rónán explained. "We don't get many visitors, but selkies are known for their hospitality, so we couldn't get rid of it. I'm glad we didn't."

Selkies known for their hospitality? Macey had a hard time not to laugh. If he knew all the stuff she'd been told about selkies.... Well, being friendly to visitors wasn't one of them.

"Macey!"

Cam came running out of the house and hugged her tight before she could even move.

"Hi, Cam," she laughed and returned the hug. "Everything okay with you?"

In response, he pressed her even tighter, running his hands over her back as if to make sure that she was real.

She stopped laughing, realising that something strange was going on.

"What's happened?" she asked softly, stroking his cheek in reassurance.

"Nightmare," he muttered. "I saw the Orca eat you, and there was nothing I could do about it. Seeing you being torn apart... I just want to chain you to myself and never let you out of my sight."

"I'm not sure I'm into bondage," she replied light-heartedly in an attempt to cheer him up. "But if you want to try it one day... I bet we can find handcuffs somewhere."

He laughed, but didn't let go of her.

"I'm here," she whispered, now serious. "I'm alive. You won't get rid of me that easily."

Before she could say any more, his lips met hers in a desperate kiss, as if he still had to convince himself that she was real.

"I'll go find Cara," Rónán laughed. "Maybe go inside, people are staring."

Macey nodded, eager to escape from the situation. Lucky for her, Cam responded instantly and pulled her inside the hut.

SEVENTEEN

"See, I told you she was okay," Jared said the moment they arrived inside. While his words seemed to be relieved, he did rush towards Macey and pull her to him, smothering her face with soft kisses.

"I didn't see you disagreeing when I said I'd go find her," Cam pointed out, still sounding a little off.

It was odd. She didn't think she'd ever witnessed him so flustered about anything. Not even when the Staran had been so sick. Maybe Self-Doubt was back again? Or was this something different even? If he was doubting her safety, then maybe the unease wasn't to do with what was within him, but what he thought of Rónán.

She didn't say a word. She didn't want to face the possibility that one of her men mistrusted another.

That would only sow more discourse and not make for a happy relationship.

"Where's Rónán?" Flint asked, as if knowing what she was thinking.

"He's gone to go deal with another selkie," Macey answered quickly, jealousy spiking within her as she recalled Cara.

"Want me to go keep an eye on them?" Jared asked.

She thought about it for a moment. While she barely knew Rónán, she did trust him and knew he wouldn't intentionally betray her. But then, she didn't trust Cara in the slightest. The woman was a grasper to say the least and if she'd steal another selkie's skin, then what else would she do?

"Yes," she whispered. "But just to make sure Rónán's okay. I don't think he'd be able to hurt another selkie if he tried, but I don't know what she's capable of."

"Got it." Jared gave her a mock salute and she smiled despite herself. She loved the incubus so much.

He kissed her forehead as he passed, trailing a hand around her waist. His touch made her shiver. When had she become so sensitive?

She twisted slightly, watching him leave longingly. It hadn't even been that long since the two of them had been together, and yet she was already craving him again.

Jared started chuckling the moment he reached the door and turned back to them. "Don't worry, Macey, Cam and Flint will take care of that craving." He winked and then ducked out once more.

"How does he do that?" she muttered.

"He's an incubus, telling when you're horny is one of his powers," Flint pointed out, a teasing grin tugging at his lips.

"Ah, yes, that." She'd known really but it was so easy to forget he was at least a little part demon. Though how much of one, she didn't really know.

"So, you up for it?" Flint waggled his eyebrows.

"With you? Always," she replied, reaching for the hem of her shirt and whipping it over her head without even waiting them to make a move. Macey wasn't in the mood for a slow steady build. She wanted hard and fast and undeniable.

"I guess that answered that one," Cam said, closing the small gap between them. "But how do you want us?" he whispered so close that his breath fanned against her skin.

"Why are you overthinking this?" she asked. "Why aren't we just going for it?"

She went onto her toes and pressed a kiss against Cam's lips, the connection between them surging into life. Macey could feel it right down to her core. How had she become this lucky? She'd always been a bit of a loner back in the Loch and she definitely hadn't had much of a love life. But here...here she had her men. She'd never be alone again. And while that should scare her, it didn't. She knew she was better with them than without. Even if it did mean she couldn't ever move back to the Loch. Not with Flint in tow.

"Good question," Flint said.

Macey sensed him behind her and relaxed into him. She was wedged between the two of them, their hot bodies pressed against hers and making a delicious Macey sandwich.

She'd certainly enjoy being in the middle of it.

Breaking the kiss with Cam, Macey twisted around and kissed Flint. The angle was slightly awkward but it meant she could kiss her man and that made it worth it.

Gently, Cam guided her body around so she was facing her Fire Warden. His hands skimmed her body, leaving a trail of goose bumps along the way. There weren't any feelings that could rival this.

She moaned into Flint's mouth just as Cam's hands reached her ass. He slipped his hands around to unbutton her jeans and help her slip them down her legs, leaving her blissfully naked for them.

Squirming a little, she pressed herself against Flint more. The two of them were wearing far more clothing than they should be but she trusted them to do something about that soon enough. They weren't the kind of men who'd pass on the opportunity.

"Now," she murmured. "Don't make me wait."

"Seems like someone's needy." Cam chuckled, nuzzling his lips against her neck as Flint moved a hand further down her body.

"I haven't been with either of you since..." she started, but was silenced by her own moaning as Flint slipped a hand between her legs and teased her gently.

"We know, Macey. We've missed you too," Flint said, a satisfied smile lighting up her face.

"We should be kind and give in to her," Cam suggested.

"Please," Macey begged.

"We got you," Flint said. "But do you trust us?"

"Of course," she answered instantly.

"Close your eyes," Cam ordered.

Without thinking, she screwed them shut. She could still feel her men close to her, their bodies touching hers. The darkness seemed to put all her nerves even more on edge and she relished it. This was new. And exciting.

Something soft brushed past her eyes and rested there. "Is that..."

"Yes," Flint answered from in front of her. "Don't try to open your eyes," he repeated.

"If you want to stop, just say voices," Cam instructed.

"Voices?" she squeaked. It seemed to be an odd choice of words.

"It's not exactly a word you'd normally scream out during sex," he pointed out. "Unless there's something you haven't told us."

"No, nothing," she said hastily.

"Then relax and let us do our thing," Flint said.

Macey nodded but said nothing. She could already feel the anticipation building within her. She didn't think she'd ever felt like this before, not even with her men before.

A hand touched her stomach before trailing across it. A second hand joined the first but she wasn't sure which belonged to which of her men. They were both standing close to her, so she guessed they were both touching her, but it was hard to tell.

"We're going to move you now," Flint whispered, not breaking the moment.

The hands disappeared and she groaned in disappointment. One of the men slipped their arms under her legs and hoisted her up, carrying her over to what she assumed what would be the bed. Though she wasn't all that sure about that. She hadn't really gotten a good look about. Cam had been a little bit to much of a mess for her to look around. She'd have to try and remember to ask him about the dream when things were a little less physical. It wasn't exactly something she wanted to deal with right now. It'd be something of a mood killer.

Whichever of the two was carrying her laid her down. The bed had been the right guess, the softness surprised her almost as much as it had the night before. How had her people ever thought badly of selkies? With beds like these, she doubted anyone would ever have a bad experience with them.

Her thoughts were interrupted by a hand sneaking up each thigh. The touches were firm, the callouses on them expected and only adding to the sensation. She wanted the two of them so badly but couldn't do anything to actually tell them other than moan.

She was nothing more than a body of sensation. Nothing mattered other than the three of them in a bed and the only thing that would have made it more perfect would be the addition of Rónán and Jared too. Though how she'd keep up with four men at once was beyond her. Saying that, she was managing emotionally, so there was little doubt she'd work it out in the bedroom too.

Maybe Jared's kabouter family wasn't too far off thinking about grandchildren.

She thrashed her head from side to side, half from the pleasure of the caresses all over her body and partly to rid herself of any thoughts of children. She wasn't ready yet. And not just because she had a world to save. There were so many other things she wanted to do and experience in life which would be a lot more difficult if she had to do it with a child in tow. Plus there were other things to work out. Like the roles of all her men in the child's life, no matter which was going to end up being the father.

Firm lips pressed against hers, while the other man parted her legs. Neither of them were being particularly gentle. Nor were they being rough. It was that perfect balance between which made Macey feel more wanted with each touch of skin on skin.

The man kissing her trailed his lips over her neck and down to her collarbone, just as the other began to move up the insides of her legs. Macey arched off the bed. They weren't even touching any of the places she wanted them and she was already a needy pile of mush.

A low moan escaped from her lips as they moved inwards. Having two men in bed with her wasn't a new experience, but something about the fact she couldn't tell who was doing what gave it a new edge. An exciting one. It was almost surprising it wasn't Jared involved this time, though given the accessibility of a blindfold, it had probably been his idea in the first place. If this was the kind of thing he was going to come up with then she was more than happy to let him be in charge of sex games.

Brief images of Jared lounging on a chair and instructing her other men in how best to pleasure her sprung to mind. Now that was something she could get on board with. Maybe she'd suggest it to him. it'd be a great feast for him if he needed to rejuvenate his powers.

Macey gave a short cry as the man between her legs settled close to her core, the sensation of his breath hitting her skin driving her higher, even if he wasn't actually touching her yet.

Sometimes, she could swear the anticipation was almost as good as the main event.

His lips caressed the inside of her thigh, almost high enough but not quite. She whimpered, just as he other man closed his lips around her nipple and rolled his tongue around it.

Her release began to coil within her body and she was worryingly close to the finish, even if her men had barely started. Not that it would stop them. All it would do was make them more determined to make her unravel several more times. They were the determined sort like that.

The kissed moved inwards, fluttering against her most sensitive places. His tongue darted out and he drew it upwards, circling it around her clit. Macey jolted, unable to keep herself still under the pressure on both her clit and her nipple at the same time,.It was times like this she was grateful for having multiple men of her own. Other women were missing out by just having the one.

A sharp pain came from her nipple as the man there tugged it between his teeth, but the pain soon subsided to a dull ache that only served to push her closer towards the edge. As if talking to each other silently, the men both increased the tempo and she couldn't hold back any longer. Letting out a piercing cry, she arched off the bed, shuddering and writhing beneath them until everything went black.

EIGHTEEN

Macey tried to blink but failed miserably. She'd almost completely blacked out and had forgotten she was wearing a blindfold. The men were still touching her, though not quite as intensely.

"Are you ready for more?" Cam asked, his voice coming from the left. Not that it told her which what he'd been doing to her before. She was pretty sure they'd moved while she'd been a little out of it.

"Yes," she said weakly. She wasn't completely convinced but knew they wouldn't push her past where she was willing to go. And it'd feel good.

So good.

"Remember when you were with us before?" Flint whispered against her skin.

"Yes," she whimpered.

"Are you ready to do it again?"

"Yes," she repeated. Almost begging, even.

Neither of them said anything else, but she felt them moving about in the bed and getting into position.

Excitement flooded through her. Before Flint and Cam, she hadn't done anything like this before. And she hadn't since either. Jared and Rónán had been far more interested in other things. She was definitely intrigued as ever and looking forward to what they had planned.

Both of them got up, probably for no other reason that to confuse her about who was doing what. She couldn't say she minded. She liked not knowing which of them was doing what, it added something else to the experience.

The bed dipped on each side as they rejoined her and one of them slipped an arm around her back and guided her into the seated position.

Lips crushed against hers. She pressed against the man in front of her and he tapped her legs so she straddled him. Naked skin met hers and she almost sighed with relief. Her men were as naked as she was now. Maybe they could finally get to the best bit.

Her inhibitions completely gone, not that they were all that prominent in the first place, she reached between them and grasped his cock in her hand, stroking up and down smoothly and enjoying the feel of it against her palm.

The man groaned and she instantly recognised it as Cam she had her legs wrapped around,. They'd been so good at keeping themselves anonymous until this second. She had to hand it to them, the blindfold was effective.

Flint ran his fingertips along her back, the tickling sensation turning her on even more than it had before.

Barely able to concentrate, she guided Cam's cock into her, glad she didn't need to see in order to do that. That alone made things so much easier.

He groaned as he pushed into her and Macey rocked back and forth, the full feeling of Cam's cock inside her already sending her higher.

After a few more thrusts, Cam gently pushed her backwards, into Flint's waiting arms. Her Fire Warden pressed his lips against hers and slipped his tongue into her mouth.

Deft fingers at the back of her head swiftly untied the blindfold, leaving it to fall away, now useless.

"You knew which of us was which anyway," Cam pointed out.

"Only at the end," she replied, pulling away from Flint a little. "But I'm glad to be able to see you now." The effort of stringing her sentence together had been a surprising amount but she didn't care. She could see them now. She would be part of this.

"Good," Flint said, running the back of one of his

fingers down her cheek in a surprisingly tender moment given how naked the three of them were.

He reached out and pulled Macey's head back to his so their lips met once more. His kisses were different this time, full of more urgency. She enjoyed the demanding side of Flint, he didn't show it quite as often as the others, but she liked when it came out to play.

"Sit on me," he instructed.

Macey nodded and straddled him as he lay down and looked up at her. Nerves fluttered in her stomach. She knew what was going to happen and she wanted it, but for some reason, she was still a little apprehensive.

"Relax, Macey," he said, stroking the insides of her thighs. She trembled, but not in fear this time.

Slowly, Flint guided himself into her while Cam watched from behind. Or at least, that was what Macey presumed he was doing. She had no real way of knowing, but the body heat he was throwing off suggested he was still close to them. Plus, she could hear his breathing and the pounding of his blood in his veins.

Pushing herself down, she took Flint into her completely. He made her feel just as full as Cam had, but in a slightly different way. It was amazing how different her men could make her feel, even if they were technically doing the same thing as before.

She cried out as he hit that place inside her which was almost too pleasurable. He slowed down in response, which just extended the blissful agony.

Leaning upwards, Flint cupped the back of her head and drew her down to him so her breasts were pressed against his chest. Her nipples scraped against his skin as they moved together in time, the sensation of which crashed through her. She was able to hold off on letting go, but only just.

Cam's hands touched her back and he trailed them down. His touch was feather light as he seemed to explore every inch of her before cupping her ass and running his finger over the crease between it and her thigh. She shivered against his touch as Flint continued to move beneath her.

Moving his hand inwards, Cam's fingers grazed across her opening, just where Flint was at the moment. He drew her wetness back and circled his fingers around the bud of her ass. Dark pleasure filled her. She knew this was seen as wrong by a lot of people, and that she probably shouldn't want it, but the part of her which begged to ignore those facts was winning at the moment and she had no desire to change that.

Slowly, Cam pushed his finger inside her. At first, her ass resisted, but Cam rubbed her lower back.

"You need to relax," he said softly.

"I'm trying," she got out through pants. She

wanted this, she really did, but it was hard to relax like he wanted when Flint was moving inside her still.

"Flint, I might need you to slow down," Cam asked through gritted teeth, his impatience making itself known a little.

"Sorry," Flint murmured, coming to a halt within her but not withdrawing. The slightest movement in any direction would remind her he was there.She was that filled by him.

Cam began to work her ass again, this time slipping his finger a little further inside her. She moaned as he circled it around and added a second finger. The burn was both uncomfortable and one of the biggest turn ons she'd ever experienced, which made the pain all the worth it. She almost couldn't wait to feel his cock buried deep inside her, but knew he had to build her up for that or it would hurt far too much.

Cam's fingers moved in and out of her faster and she bucked against Flint beneath her, who let out a groan.

"Macey, please don't do that," he managed to ask, though he didn't seem too convinced either way.

She tried to still herself but was writhing again in seconds. Flint's cock and Cam's fingers together were creating too many sensations for her to deal with. If she wasn't careful, one single movement would be enough to send her over the edge and she wasn't quite ready for this to end yet.

"I think she's ready," Flint said through bated breath.

"I think so too," Cam replied, an eager note in his voice.

He withdrew his fingers from her ass and a disappointed whine slipped from Macey as she was left feeling so empty. Her protests were cut short seconds later when he pressed his cock against her ass.

Needing him more than she wanted to admit, Macey pushed back, urging him onward. The burn returned as his cock pushed past the ring of her ass. Cam moved slowly, but within a couple of minutes, he was fully seated within her.

Neither of her men moved as the three of them got used to their positions. She hadn't felt this full since they'd done this last time, but needed to catch her breath before they continued.

In unison, the two men began to move gently, rocking in and out of her with a caution which she knew would disappear soon. It wasn't that their care for her would disappear, but from experience, she knew they'd all get caught up in what they were doing.

When they didn't speed up quite quick enough for her, she began to thrust back and forth between them, hoping they'd get the message.

Both men were hitting just the right spot, eliciting whimpers and moans from her as she came close to her peak once more. She tried to hold off for as long as she could, but it was too much and she began to shudder and quake between her men.

Sensing her impending release, the two of them picked up their own paces.

Pleasure crashed through her just as she felt the two men begin their own releases. The three of them writhed together before collapsing into a tangled heap and slipping into a deep sleep.

NINETEEN

"Macey?" Jared shouted, rushing into the room. "I see you had fun then." His whole demeanour changed as he took in the three of them tangled in bed.

"What?" Macey mumbled, her eyes barely cracked open. She barely had the energy to think and it was all Cam and Flint's fault.

But they could do it again. Any time they wanted to. She'd take it any time.

"I think Rónán needs your help," he said.

She sat bolt upright, worried for her man. "What?" she demanded again.

"He doesn't seem to be getting anywhere with Cara. She just keeps coming on to him."

"She keeps doing what?" Macey hissed.

"Coming on to him."

"I heard you." She glared at no one in particular.

No one should be coming on to her men. No one. Not even the perfect selkie, Cara. "What do you need me for?"

"She's clearly not going to give him his skin back, so we need to get it another way."

"Do you even know where it is?" Flint asked, sitting up more slowly than Macey had.

"Not really, no. I'd ask Rónán, but he's busy being flirted with."

Macey's scowl deepened but Jared didn't really seem to notice. Flint did. He rubbed her back soothingly, which she had to admit actually helped.

"Do you have a plan?" she asked.

"Not as such," he admitted. "They're stood in front of Cara's house and the only other way in is through the chimney..."

"And you want me to do the Air thing and float down into it," Macey said, giving him a look that she hoped he took as him being completely crazy.

"Pretty much, yes."

"Great, okay then."

"Good, we'll get going." Jared turned around without waiting for Macey to confirm and she frowned. Was he seriously going to walk away while she was completely naked?

"Right..."

"We don't have much time," he said.

"What makes you say that?" she asked, noticing

he hadn't actually walked away, just turned his back. That was odd behaviour for Jared, though maybe she just wasn't with it properly yet. Cam and Flint really must have done something to her brain. Was there such a thing as losing brain power from too much sex? If not, then she might be the first patient ever.

"Just a hunch." Jared shrugged and Macey sighed in response. Ignoring hunches was normally a bad sign.

"Fine. Cam, Flint, can you go find Amber and Izban and make sure they're ready to leave. Jared and I will go steal back Rónán's seal skin, grab him and then come join you by the bonfire."

"Not a good meeting spot," Jared said. "It's right by Cara's house."

"Alright then, where do you suggest?"

"Did you see the stone hut when we came into the village?" Flint asked.

"Yes." She'd noticed it because it was different from the driftwood homes the selkies seemed to favour. It had seemed a little out of place, though she hadn't thought too much of it. Her whole world was a little bit out of place.

"That's where we should meet. There's an entry to the Staran there," he said.

"Okay, that sounds like a good getaway plan. If anyone asks what the four of you are doing, tell them we have a Wardens ritual to do or something."

Cam snickered slightly, but didn't move from his spot on the bed. "Funny how you didn't even want to believe you were a Warden at one point. Now you're using it as an excuse."

"I can't exactly deny it now," Macey muttered, scooting herself away from the warm embrace of the two men in bed and towards where she hoped her clothes were.

She scooped up her clothes from where they'd been discarded all over the floor and threw them back on, not giving a second thought to how she looked.

"Right then. Let's go," she said to Jared, leaving the other two completely behind.

SHE COULDN'T HELP IT, she had to see how Rónán was getting on. Peering around the side of Cara's hut, she was just in time to see him pull a face and narrowly avoid the female selkie's forced embrace again.

Some of the jealousy within Macey settled down. He wasn't going to abandon her for this woman. Not when he was looking so displeased about being in her company.

"Macey," Jared hissed. "Not now."

"Sorry," she shot back. "But I have more at stake than just a seal skin."

"I know, but the sooner we get that skin, the sooner he'll be out of her clutches for good."

She frowned, hating he was right.

"What do I need to do?"

"I was hoping you knew that. You made the disk we travelled down to the sea on, right?"

"I suppose." Macey pondered what to do. On the one hand, she had Air magic within her. On the other, she had absolutely no idea what to do with that magic or how to wield it. Every time she'd used it so far, it had been about using it or dying. And apparently the Air Warden came with some kind of self-preservation mode installed. Admittedly, that was pretty helpful.

She clasped her hands together and concentrated on calling out to the other Warden.

Talia? I need your help.

She didn't get an answer. She hadn't really expected to.

Dismissing her first plan, she had to think fast. This had to work. One of her men was in danger, if Air wasn't going to work, then she'd find a different way.

Clasping her hands together, she focused on her water magic, calling it to the surface and picturing a geyser. She'd never made one appear before, but if she could create a whirlpool, then a spurt of water into the air should be nothing. She didn't even have to worry too much about making things wet. The selkies were water creatures anyway and Flint was far enough away not to even get hit.

Water shot up from beneath her, catapulting her into the air. All she had to do now was get off at the right point. Well, and hope there wasn't anyone about to watch the geyser and come investigate the cause. If they did, she just had to hope Jared would turn on his incubus charm and they'd forget what they were looking for. It was probably a good thing he'd have been able to snack on the residual sexual energy she'd created with Flint and Cam.

When the water was about the same height as the roof, she leapt off it, landing lithely on the roof and somehow managing to avoid falling.

A quick climb took her to the chimney pot, which was mercifully a large one and big enough to fit a small person down.

Trying not to think about it, Macey threw herself through the chimney and landed on the floor with a slight crash and jarring her ankle. There wasn't enough pain for it to be broken and she doubted it'd even be a sprain. But it would probably ache in the morning. Still worth it if it meant she could save one of her men.

Limping slightly, she looked around the surprisingly small hut. It wasn't unlike the one Rónán had taken her to, with a sleep section separated by a screen.

"If I was a power grabbing bitch, where would I keep the skin of the man I wanted to love me," Macey asked herself, realising just how crazy she sounded. No one would believe her situation if she told them, it just kept getting weirder by the second.

Closing her eyes, she listened to her gut and crept around behind the sleep screen. If it was her and she wanted someone to love her who didn't already, she'd keep the skin as close to her as possible. And if that wasn't actually on her person...

Her eyes fell to Cara's pillow and she snatched it up. Despite having an inkling it was there, Macey was surprised to actually spot the pendent lying under where the pillow had been.

She picked it up carefully and turned it over in her hands. It was smaller than she'd expected and smoother. There also didn't seem to be much power coming from it, which surprised her. She'd have thought it'd contain at least a little bit of it since it allowed the selkies to shift, but maybe it was because she couldn't use it herself that she couldn't sense it.

She dropped the pillow back into place, hoping that Cara wasn't the kind who checked on it every hour or so. If she did, then they didn't have long to get away. Turning, she looked for an escape route but found none. It was either back up the chimney or out of the front door. Somehow, the latter option seemed the safest. If she created a geyser in here and left it flooded, it'd be a dead giveaway that there was something up.

She crept forward, reaching the front door a little sooner than she would have liked. Peering through it, she spotted Rónán and Cara talking, with the former appearing more and more agitated by the moment. Even so, she couldn't tell what they were saying. Probably because they seemed to be talking in selkie language rather than in English.

Cara's back was to her. As long as she was quiet, she could get out of the house without raising any suspicions. Maybe.

Deciding there was no time like the present, she slipped through the door and hugged the side of the hut. She needed to get back to Jared and then approach Rónán from a different angle. That way, she could avoid at least a little suspicion.

She was too busy paying attention to the selkies that she ran straight into Jared's chest as she rounded the side of the hut.

"Oomf." The sound escaping from Jared sounded almost painful, though she doubted he was really hurt. It would take more than someone of her tiny frame to make a dent in Jared.

"We need to hurry," she whispered.

"You got it?" he replied.

She nodded rather than saying anything.

Holding out her hand, she was relieved when he took it.

The two of them began a leisurely stroll towards where the selkies were standing. They didn't have very far to go, but hopefully it'd be enough to look convincing.

"Rónán!" Macey called.

The selkies turned to look at her, one with a smile, the other with a glare. It seemed Macey wasn't the only one with jealousy issues.

"Everything okay?" Rónán asked.

"Yes. But we need your advice on something back at the hut." She smiled sweetly, hoping he'd get the message and that it would annoy Cara. Two birds with one stone and all that jazz. Or maybe she should use two seals with one stone. Though that did sound unnecessarily violent.

"You do?" He cocked his head to the side, a puzzled look on his face.

"Yes, urgently." She tried to put as much of an explanation into her eyes as possible, but worried he hadn't known her long enough to pick up on that.

Indecision warred over his face before he nodded. "Okay, coming. Thank you for your time, Cara."

"We weren't done," the female selkie protested.

"Yes, we were," Rónán replied. "I'll see you later."

He turned away from the woman and closed the distance between him and Macey.

"You okay?" she asked him when he was close enough for her to whisper to.

"Yes. Are you? What's the problem?"

"Not here," Macey whispered, grabbing his hand and pulling him away from Cara's hut.

When they were far enough away for it to be safe, Macey pressed his necklace into his hand. Rónán's eyes widened in disbelief. "Is it? It is!" Joy lit up his face as he opened his palm and studied the necklace. "Thank you." He looked at both Macey and Jared with clear wonder on his face.

"You're welcome," Macey replied, going up on her toes and giving him a swift kiss.

"You're part of the team," Jared added. "We protect the team." He shrugged as if that was all there was to it and Macey supposed that was true.

"Even so, thank you," the selkie said.

"We should probably get going though. I don't want to even consider what Cara will do when she discovers it gone."

"Where even was it?" Jared asked.

"In her bed," Macey replied.

The incubus let out a hearty chuckle. "The one place Rónán would never have gone willingly."

"Too damn right, I wouldn't," Rónán muttered

darkly while slipping the necklace over his head so it settled on his chest. He sighed with relief.

"Now...to the others?" Jared prompted.

"Yes, to the others," Macey acknowledged.

"ABOUT TIME," Flint called as they approached the stone building. "I was starting to get worried."

"No you weren't," Jared countered. "It's barely been an hour."

"That's still long enough," Cam said. "We should probably get going."

"I agree." Macey glanced over her shoulder, still half expecting to see Cara storming towards them with a murderous look on her face. "Does anyone actually know where we should be going next?"

"Wherever the Mahoun is?" Amber suggested.

"If that means the Keep then count me out," Macey replied. "But do we really want to go into the Staran and ask them to take us to Mahoun? I can come up with a dozen reasons why that's a terrible idea."

The others thought for a moment.

"What about going back to the house and thinking there?" Flint suggested. "We'll be more comfortable, there's less risk of an angry kelpie suddenly appearing and Rónán can go for the shifted swim I'm sure he's longing to go for."

"Please," Rónán responded. "It's been a long time."

Macey rested a hand on his arm, trying to send him as much comfort as she could. Spending that long without shifting was pure torture. She could completely understand why he wanted to swim. Plus, she also wanted to see him in his selkie form. She longed to see the graceful and powerful way she was sure he could swim.

"Yes, let's do that," Macey agreed. "We can make a better plan then."

The others agreed and she prepared herself to travel the Staran again. Though this time she'd be with Flint and Cam who'd travelled dozens of times before.

They all linked hands and they stepped towards them. But the closer they got, the greater Macey's sense of foreboding grew. Somewhere deep within her, she was convinced the Staran weren't going to let them out quite where they wanted to go.

TWENTY

They were thrown out of the Staran in a tangle of limbs.

"What the bleeding waves was that?" Macey asked breathlessly, struggling to sit up. "That's never happened before."

Her head was spinning and she had to blink several times for her vision to return to normal. Only then did she see where they'd landed.

She gasped.

Seven stone thrones surrounded them, the same ones they'd sat at when they'd defeated Self-Doubt.

"Why are we here?" Amber whispered into the empty room, scrambling to her feet. "What are we supposed to do here?"

They gathered in the centre of the room, all

slightly unsteady on their feet from the turbulent journey on the Staran.

"Why did they bring us here?" Cam muttered, walking over to the throne that had his name carved into the headrest.

Rónán cleared his throat. "While you all seem to know this place, I have no clue. Anybody want to fill me in?"

Macey took his hand and led him to the throne bearing her name. "These are the Wardens' seats. We've been here once before, when we defeated Self-Doubt. Back then, we had help though. Now, I have no idea what to do or why we're even here."

Suddenly, blue flames flickered into existence above each of the thrones. Macey jumped back, her water magic roaring to life inside of her, ready to fight the fire. She smothered her powers, somehow knowing that these flames weren't there to harm them.

"What the...." Flint exclaimed and reached out to touch the fire, but before he got close enough, the flames disappeared as if they'd never been there in the first place.

"Well, that was anticlimactic," Izban drawled, but then his eyes widened and he picked something up from his throne. "Look, there are notes!"

Macey checked her own throne, and there it was, a tiny, scorched piece of parchment.

KELPIES.

That didn't make any sense. She knew that she was a kelpie, she didn't need a mysterious message to tell her that.

"Kabouters and kludde," Jared read aloud.

"Ceasg," Amber said, looking at her piece of paper just as cluelessly as Macey felt.

It turned out that they all had a different species on their parchments. Cam had na fir ghorma, the storm kelpies, Flint had the sìth and Izban had...

"Prophets?" he asked incredulously. "How many prophets do we know besides Malan?"

Macey frowned. "The cù sìth gave me a prophecy, but she's dead. Unless she's returned as a ghost dog, Malan style."

"Fedelm!" Amber exclaimed. "The woman who met us at the pub when we went to see Nessie. Who brought our men back to us."

She blushed a little, probably thinking of how she'd reunited with Izban by snogging a lot.

"I never even properly met her," Izban complained. "She appeared out of nowhere, told us to follow her, and then suddenly we were in a pub in Scotland. She never even told us her name. Why am I the one who's got to find the prophets?"

"Wait, what do you mean? Find them?" Cam asked, looking at the mage thoughtfully. "Are you thinking that we each need to find the people on our papers?"

Izban groaned in frustration. "Am I the only one who can see the obvious? Those are all friends and allies we've met over the past few months. Whoever brought us here, whoever sent us these messages, they want us to find them and probably get them to help us defeat the Mahoun. They know we can't do it on our own. Just because we're the Seven Wardens doesn't mean that we have to fight the Voice alone."

"Wow, he's actually talking sense," Jared snickered, but immediately shut up when the mage shot him a very dark look. He turned serious. "What do we do when we find and convince them to help us? We still don't know where the Mahoun is or how to get to him. Or how to fight him, even. As much as I like the idea of getting our allies together, this isn't a very good plan."

"The Staran brought us here," Macey said thoughtfully. "And now we got these messages. Someone is helping us. Should we just assume that they'll keep helping us? Should we trust them to bring us to the Mahoun when the time is right?"

Flint shook his head. "I don't like this. This could all be one gigantic trap by the Voice to split us up and then capture us one by one. So far, the only person who's occasionally helped us is Malan. Why would someone else suddenly start assisting us without even introducing themselves?"

"Maybe it's Malan." Jared shrugged. "He loves playing games, maybe he just wants to make it all more interesting."

Macey huffed. "Well, if this was him, he's certainly managed to confuse us. Not that he ever not confuses us. He's never said a straight sentence to me, not one simple, easy to understand word of advice." She paused for a moment and twirled her piece of paper between her fingers. "But I don't think this is Malan. He wouldn't want to miss seeing the confusion on our faces. He loves to show off, while this is someone who doesn't want to be seen or thanked. A mystery benefactor. Or, as Flint said, a trap."

"We were eventually going to ask for help from our friends anyway, weren't we," Amber said, absent-mindedly reaching out for Izban who took her hand. "Maybe this is intended to give us a little push in that direction."

Macey ran her hands through her hair. She really didn't know what to think. There were so many possibilities and questions racing through her mind, but none of them stood out as the solution to this strange riddle. What Flint had said made sense. The Voice had tried to split them up before, and had managed to capture Macey in the process. Still, that theory didn't sit right with her. The way the messages had appeared in the flames... that was a beautiful, intricate magic, and she couldn't imagine the Mahoun wielding that kind of power. His magic was likely more crude, more violent.

"Let's go in pairs," she decided. "That way we can go everywhere quickly, but aren't alone." When nobody protested, she quickly continued. "Cam and I both have water beings, so we'll go together. Izban and Amber, I don't think I'll even try and split you up. That leaves Flint and Jared. Rónán didn't get a mission, but maybe it would be best for you to join Amber? Maybe the ceasg will appreciate a selkie coming to visit."

She didn't want to say that it was a bad idea for Rónán to come with her. As liberal as her family were, they probably wouldn't like her bringing a selkie back home. Especially not her selkie boyfriend.

He seemed to understand, giving her a smile and a nod.

"What are we going to do exactly?" Jared asked. "I'm sure the kabouters are going to support us, but where are we going to meet? Am I to ask all their best warriors to come with me? Or just their mages? Who do we need?" He sighed. "Why is everything so complicated?"

Macey shrugged. She didn't know any more than the incubus did. "The Staran brought us here. Let's ask it to bring us where we need to go? And if it doesn't, let's meet at Malan's house. He'll probably lead us in the right direction just to get rid of us."

Jared chuckled. "Yes, you may be right about that. Maybe I'll pick up some waffles for him while we're in Belgium. If we don't see the prophet, we can always offer them to the Mahoun. Maybe he'll give up in return for waffles."

"This is getting silly," Izban growled. "Let's go. I wish our phones worked here but as they don't, let's leave a message with Malan should something happen."

He stepped towards the large door they'd come through, pulling Amber with him.

She waved at Macey, unperturbed by her boyfriend's sour demeanour. "See you later!"

As soon as the couple had stepped through the door, they disappeared, swallowed by the strange magic surrounding this place. Macey walked over to Cam, who was staring intently at his piece of paper.

"I'm not exactly looking forward to visiting the storm kelpies again," he admitted. "Shall we go to your family first?"

"Yes." Macey nodded grimly. "I have a loch monster to talk to."

～

THE LOCH WAS COVERED in thick fog that seemed to suck in the last evening light. It didn't make sense to Macey that it was almost night here already, but she remembered how the guys had told her once that time flowed differently on Earth than it did on the other planes.

The Staran had released them at the very tip of the loch, not far from where the underwater palace was based. Problem was that she couldn't actually take Cam down there.

"I'll try and call my aunt," Macey explained while she undressed. "She's the one with the best hearing, so hopefully she'll send my father up here without me having to swim all the way down to his home."

Cam nodded, but his eyes were fixed on her naked skin. "You've got scales again," he said softly, pointing to her abdomen.

He was right. Hundreds of tiny scales were covering her belly and thighs, sparkling whenever she moved. Strange. They seemed to come and go as they wanted. She shrugged. A problem for another day.

She stepped into the cool water, immediately feeling happier. This was home. The familiar smell of the loch calmed her mind and she breathed in deep, relaxing further. She needed to come here more often. Now that she was swimming in the loch, she noticed how much she'd missed it.

She dived, her eyes quickly adjusting to the dim

light filtering through the water's smooth surface. She knew she only needed to partly shift, but she couldn't resist shifting all the way. As soon as her gills had sprung up along her neck, she breathed in the cool water, relishing in the refreshment it brought.

Home.

She took another deep breath, then started to shout in kelpie, loudly clicking in the way only her kind understood. She was calling Nessie's name as loud as she could, again and again, until she finally got a reply. The clicks were too far away to understand, but it was enough to know that someone had heard her and was on the way.

Macey waited, treading water, wishing she could go for a proper swim and visit her relatives. She'd always been an independent kelpie, especially when she moved onto land, but still, she loved her family.

"Maaaceeeyyyy!"

The waves of the loch elongated the call and she couldn't help but smile. It wasn't Nessie who was coming to meet her. It was her father.

He was a large kelpie and didn't just have one, but two antennae protruding from his forehead. It was the sign that he was the king, the most powerful of them all. Kelpie monarchy was only partly hereditary. If a kelpie with two antennae was born, it was usually raised in the Royal family as the crown prince or princess. Neither Macey nor her two brothers had two of the strange sense organs, so if a two-antannaed baby was to be born just now, they'd slip down one place in the line to the throne. Macey didn't really care; she'd never aspired to be queen.

Right now, the king's antennae were twitching as he approached his daughter.

"You brought a friend?" he asked as way of greeting, before gently nuzzling his head against hers. "Is he more than a friend?"

"Dad!" Macey flicked her tail at him. "Behave. He's not met any other kelpies yet, so please don't traumatise him."

The king laughed heartily. "It's good to see you, my daughter. I assume this isn't just a family visit?"

His large eyes turned a little sad and Macey regretted that she hadn't been able to come for a normal visit in such a long time. Right now, she'd love to dive down to the palace, play games with her father, steal treats from the cook, check on her algae collection. But no, she had to save the world. The responsibility was weighing hard on her shoulders, but she also felt like a bit of a fool. How was she, Macey, a loch kelpie, supposed to do something so monumental? She had no clue of what she was actually doing, or what she had to do to succeed. It was all just one big mess that nobody was going to clean up but herself.

"I've missed you," she whispered, rubbing against her father in a hug. "There's a lot I need to tell you."

"I'm listening."

She shook her head. "Let's return to the surface so Cam can join the conversation."

"Cam? That's his name? I'm having trouble sensing what he is."

She smiled. "A wraith."

"Oh. Not met many of those. There used to be a wraith couple running a pub in Inverness, a long time before you were born, but..."

"Dad?"

He chuckled. "Sorry. A story for another time. I'll half-shift, if you don't mind. I don't want to show my future wraith-in-law my naked human form."

Macey swallowed hard, but decided not to comment. It was better that way. Her father had a strange kind of humour, and she couldn't put it past him to shift and go talk to Cam while being completely naked.

Kelpies were used to nudeness when shifting, but she'd learned quickly that other species weren't the same. She was so used to the human sense of modesty that she was almost ashamed to shift and return to Cam naked.

She shook off the embarrassing thoughts and began the shift, slowly changing from kelpie to human. The moment her gills disappeared, she broke the surface and took in a big gasp of air.

"Everything okay?" Cam called from the banks of the loch, quite a distance away.

Instead of answering, she swam to him with strong, fast strides, reaching him much faster than a normal human swimmer would have been able to. It was part of her kelpie magic.

"Who's that?" Cam asked while she was leaving the water, searching for her clothes. Cam handed her her shirt which he'd carefully folded over his arm. He was such a gentleman.

"My father," Macey muttered. "He's the king but just behave normally. He doesn't expect formality from non-kelpies."

Cam nodded, apprehension showing in his features. While Macey had met Jared's adoptive parents, this was the first time one of the guys met her family.

"Is he going to come outside?"

Macey pulled up her jeans and slipped into her shoes. Her feet hadn't dried yet and she sighed at the squeaky feeling that she was going to have to deal with for the next hour or so.

"No, he's going to stay half-shifted," she explained. "Dad, meet Cam!" she called out and her father swam closer to the shore. His torso was human, but his back and legs were kelpie. He looked a bit like a centaur, Macey thought with a smile.

"Cam, this is my father, Ahearn, King of the Kelpies."

"It's good to meet you, sir," Cam said politely, doing something that was probably supposed to be a half bow.

"And you. I hear you are a wraith? Are you perchance related to Isabella and Victor McCloughan from Inverness?"

Cam shook his head. "No, at least I don't think so. I'm adopted, so I don't know who I'm related to."

"I'm sure I could ask them..."

"Dad," Macey interrupted. "We need your help."

The kelpie king's expression immediately sobered.

"Are you pregnant?"

Macey laughed. "You know you're the second person who's asked me that this week?"

Her father raised his bushy eyebrows. "Who was the first?"

"A kabouter woman... don't even ask. Has Aunt Nessie told you what I discussed with her?"

He nodded solemnly. "The Wardens business? Aye, she has. I'm still having trouble imagining my little foal having such responsibility. But if anyone can do it, you can."

Macey's eyes began to sting and she blinked away her tears.

"That's why we're here," she said quickly before she began to get emotional. "We're preparing to fight the Mahoun, the entity that has taken on the shape of the devil, and we need as much help as we can get. The other Wardens are travelling to other communities to recruit allies, but of course I came here first."

"Of course," her father repeated. "Anything you need. You know we're no warriors, but I will give you my best mages. I would come myself, but we've been having trouble recently... No, I don't want to add to your problems. If my theory is correct, this is related to the evilness that is overtaking the world. If you defeat the Mahoun, maybe it will get better."

Macey was about to say something, to protest that she needed to know, but Cam was quicker.

"Thank you. We'll take whoever you can spare. And once we're done, we'll return and help. Right, Macey?"

Again, she wanted to protest, but she knew he was right. She couldn't start fighting on yet another front. The Mahoun had to be their priority.

"Can you call them now?" she asked her father. "We need to leave again soon. We can drop them in the place where we'll meet the other Wardens. Then we'll have to travel to the na fir ghorma."

Ahearn looked at her in astonishment. "The storm kelpies? You're going to meet the storm kelpies?"

Macey smiled. "We've visited them before. Their crown prince is quite nice, actually. Their king is slightly deluded, but they did offer their help, so now we're going to take them up on that."

The kelpie king shook his head. "I'm not quite sure what to think of that. I better get the mages."

He shifted in one fluid motion, far quicker than Macey could.

Before he dived, he clicked a question and Macey couldn't help but laugh.

"No, I'm not!"

Na Fir Ghorma (Blue Men of the Minch)

TWENTY-ONE

They left their twenty kelpie mages at Malan's hut. The prophet didn't look surprised at all, and just told them to come inside for some tea. The kelpie's were all slightly bewildered, but they trusted their princess to have a reason for bringing them there. None of the other Wardens had arrived yet, so Macey scribbled down a quick message for them to say that they were now headed to the na fir ghorma. Half of their task done already. So far, this was going surprisingly well.

She was a little worried about the others, but they were all capable people and hadn't been selected as Wardens just for anything. They could do it. And it wasn't a trap. No. It couldn't be. Macey wouldn't allow it.

"Ready?" Cam asked, putting an arm around her shoulders. It was only early afternoon in Malan's domain and he'd given them some oatcakes as a midday snack. Macey was nibbling on hers, trying not to worry.

"Aye, let's go and see the storm kelpies. Let's hope they don't expect us to feast with them again."

Macey shuddered at the thought of the food they'd been served at their last visit. And the king... well, hopefully he'd recovered from the shock that the sìth had deceived him for decades, if not longer, by pretending that they'd built the Staran just for the storm kelpies.

She willed the Staran into existence rather than let Cam do it. She needed the practice, after all, and she was beginning to find it surprisingly easy. The trick seemed to be imagining travelling on the Staran, and then they were there. It was weird and didn't quite make sense. But what in this magical world did.

"To the na fir ghorma," Macey whispered, hoping that the Staran would somehow drop them in the underwater city of the storm kelpies and not in the middle of the ocean. That wouldn't be a problem for her, but Cam wouldn't be able to hold his breath for long enough to dive all the way down to the ocean floor.

They stepped onto the Staran and were swallowed by the mists...

... and were slammed against a barrier.

"What the rotten kelp is happening?" Macey

cursed, shoving Cam off her before he squeezed her to death. It felt like the Staran had deposited them against a glass wall, but it was too misty to see anything.

"Hello?" Cam shouted, hammering against the barrier.

Guards! A muffled noise came from the other side and hurried footsteps approached the barrier.

A bang against the wall vibrated through Macey's body. *Who's there? How did you get in?* a rough voice shouted in their minds. Well, that at least answered the question whether they were in the right place.

"Get in? We're not really in," Cam muttered.

"My name is Macey, Princess of the Kelpies. I am here to see the Crown Prince, Muahwa. Can you let us in?"

More shuffling, then another knock against the barrier.

Macey? Is that really you?

Suddenly, the barrier dissolved and they fell into the room, Cam landing once again on Macey.

"Get off me, you ogre," she grumbled, the wind knocked out of her.

"Wraith, not ogre. We smell better." He shot her a grin and helped her up.

Princess, we welcome you.

She turned to see Muahwa, his bright blue skin

glistening in the light of the glowfish placed above the glass ceiling.

He bowed formally, but then, without warning, he flung himself at her, hugging her tightly.

"Ehm..."

Macey was speechless, but Cam cleared his throat, pulling the na firm ghorma off her. Muahwa looked a little sheepish and a dark blue spread over his cheeks.

You healed the Staran. The storms have calmed. We are in your debt.

The prince bowed again, back to his normal formal self.

Was it the sith? he asked, and Macey remembered how the storm kelpies had suspected the seelie of messing with the Staran.

"No," she shook her head, "it was something else. The same reason why we're now here. Could we talk to the king, please?"

The blue blush on Muahwa's cheeks spread.

You're talking to him.

Macey took a step back. "What?"

My father died last month. I'm the king now.

She noticed her mouth was still hanging wide open and quickly closed it. She hadn't expected that, not at all.

"Long live the king," Cam muttered and to their

surprise, the guards standing at the door on the other side of the room repeated the phrase in their minds.

"I'm so sorry," Macey said gently, noticing the sad look on the blue man's face. "How did he die?"

He tried to travel on the Staran. We all told him it was too dangerous, but he wouldn't listen. He was torn apart.

Muahwa opened his giant mouth and made a strange sound. It touched something deep inside of Macey and almost made her cry. It was probably the saddest sound she'd ever heard, made by a being that didn't use their voices to talk.

"I am sorry," Macey repeated.

It can't be undone. But why are you here? I'm sure you didn't come so I could thank you?

"No..." She didn't really want to ask for help now that she knew that his father had died, but there was no other way. They needed the support. She sighed and quickly explained what had been feeding on the Staran and how the Mahoun was a relative of that evil creature.

So this devil is stronger than the being you already defeated?

Macey nodded. "Yes, we think so. He's managed to reach and affect so many people, and he's been scheming for a long time. He's also got my brothers and I don't know if they're still alive."

She pressed a hand over her mouth. She hadn't intended to say that. Macey didn't want to make it sound so personal. She wasn't just doing this for herself and for her family. She really did want to defeat the Mahoun so that the entire world would be safer again.

The na fir ghorma put a blue hand on her arm.

I understand. We will help.

"Really? I am... we are grateful," she stuttered, distracted by how sad the blue man's eyes were. As if he wasn't just sad for his own, but also for her loss, and that of everybody else. She no longer found him ugly like she had when she'd first met him. Yes, his giant mouth was creepy and his skin was... well, blue, but that didn't matter. The inside mattered.

We won't be able to leave the sea for long. We will need to stay close to the Staran which connects us to our home. If you fight far away from it, we won't be able to follow, but we can secure a path of retreat, should it be necessary.

"Hopefully not," Macey muttered, before lifting her voice. "I thank you, King Muahwa. We are in your debt."

Not at all. You calmed the storms. Our home would be in danger without you.

She smiled at him. "Let's just agree that we're doing a good job helping each other."

He nodded. *I will prepare my warriors. Where shall I send them?*

"We're gathering at the prophet Malan's house. Do you know where that is?"

The blue man nodded. *The Staran will show us the way.*

"Good. We better get back and see where the others are. How do we get out of here?"

Muahwa laughed in their minds. *I'll lower the barrier. Next time, just knock and I'll let you in.*

As if it was that easy. She shook her head in amusement and stepped into the Staran, holding Cam's hand. They'd completed their missions. How were the others faring?

TWENTY-TWO

Chaos awaited them. Malan's front garden, usually a quiet and almost boring place, was full of people. Macey waved to some of her father's kelpie mages who lifted their hands in greeting in return. The na fir ghorma stayed close to the mists they'd stepped out of, sceptically looking at the other assembled people.

A group of kabouter were sitting in the garden and Macey had to hide her grin. They looked suspiciously like garden gnomes. Jared was amongst them, talking to Jerimiah and another kabouter that looked very similar. His brother, maybe?

When the incubus met Macey's glance, he got up and ran towards her, hugging her as soon as she was in reach.

"Good to see you," he muttered against the nape

of her neck, his breath hot on her skin. His incubus powers were pushing against her nerves and she could feel the arousal tingle through her.

"Power it down a little?" she asked in something that was close to a moan.

"Sorry." He grinned. "I was just a little worried. Did the storm kelpies give you any trouble?"

Macey looked back at the small group of blue people. It was mostly men, but there were three women as well. "Nope, they're harmless. Long story, but Muahwa is now their new king, and he was very happy to send some of his warriors to help us. Did everything go okay with the kabouters and kludde?"

Jared grimaced. "Kabouters, yes, they sent two dozen people and more are on their way. The kludde... not so much." He sighed deeply. "Their powers are out of control. Wilg said it wasn't safe for any of them to come and help. Not even he himself felt like his magic was stable enough to be of much use. He did show me a vision though."

His expression darkened. "I'm not allowed to tell you about it until the time has come."

"What time?" Macey asked in confusion.

He winked and pretended to zip his lips shut, but his eyes stayed sad. "No chance. Not telling you. Amber and Izban just returned, shall we check on them?"

She was very aware that he'd brazenly changed

the topic, but the look in his eyes made her stop asking any more questions.

They walked over to the other side of the grassy area where Amber and Izban were standing by themselves. Rónán had disappeared. When the beithir saw them approach, she waved, but it was a weak gesture.

Macey increased her steps. "What happened?" she asked as soon as she was close enough for them to hear her.

Macey shrugged. "No water, no ceasg. Having Rónán with us didn't help, she just said she couldn't assist us."

"And Fedelm refused to come as well. She said she was needed somewhere else," Izban said with a drawn-out sigh. "It was a waste of time."

Several stones dropped into Macey's stomach. Somehow she'd hoped the ceasg would be able to join them. She'd seemed like a good ally to have, but she didn't seem to be able to shift and walk on land like her and the selkies did.

"Salty seaweed," Macey muttered in frustration, but Cam started to laugh.

"What did you just say?"

"Salty seaweed," Macey repeated with a pout. "It's a well-known kelpie curse."

Jared snickered. "Seriously? It's a bit tame."

Izban didn't smile like the others. "Have you seen

the others? Rónán went to get some food, but I've not spotted Flint."

Wait, wasn't Flint supposed to be with Jared?

Macey turned and looked back at the crowd assembled behind them. The incubus was walking towards them, deep in conversation with Jerimiah.

"Jared!" Macey called. "Where's Flint?"

"He said he was preparing a surprise!" Jared shouted back. "He should be somewhere in Malan's house."

"And the seelie?"

Jared shook his head. "Two of them talked to us in front of their city walls, but they didn't even let us in. We waited for a bit to see if one of the sìth who helped us last time would come out, but they didn't."

"Another waste of time," Izban muttered darkly.

"What kind of surprise?" Macey asked. A strange feeling was overtaking her, the urge to run and search for Flint.

"One of the seelie gave him something." Jared shrugged. "A present for you. He didn't let me see it, and he went straight inside when we arrived back here, letting me deal with the kabouters."

"One doesn't 'deal' with kabouters," Jerimiah corrected. "One is honoured to get the attention of kabouters."

Macey smiled but it didn't reach her heart.

"I'll go look for him," she said, already on the way

to the house. She could feel her men follow her, but she didn't look back. Something was wrong.

The door was wide open and a clutter of kabouters was standing in the entrance hall, nibbling on biscuits Malan had apparently provided. She'd not seen the prophet yet, but right now, she didn't care.

Instinctively, she turned to the right and ran up the stairs. There were five doors on this floor, but she knew exactly which one to take.

She opened it and cried out.

Flint was on the ground, blood pooling around his hand which was clutching a fiery red stone. His eyes were wide open but unseeing, rings of flames burning around his pupils.

"Flint!" Macey shouted and fell to her knees by his side. He didn't react. Tears were streaming down his face, his expression was torn in agony, but he didn't make a sound or even move.

A smell of burning came from his hand and it took Macey a moment to see that the stone that she'd thought was red was actually burning with tiny flames. It was like a piece of white-red coal but much sharper and definitely not natural.

This was magic, bad magic.

His skin around the stone was blistering, but Flint's grip on it was tight.

"Flint!" She shook his shoulders, but he didn't react at all.

"Use your water!" Cam shouted from behind her and she stretched out an arm, shooting water at Flint's burning hand. The water turned into steam the moment it hit the stone, filling the air with an acrid smell.

A blast of air dispelled the steam. The stone had stopped burning, but Flint was still keeping it gripped tight in his fist. Carefully, Macey reached out to touch his hand, but before she could, the stone suddenly glowed again, a strange white-silver that blinded her and judging from the shouts, all the others too. She shielded her eyes with both hands until the light lessened.

The stone was gone. All that remained was Flint's empty, burned hand, the blisters black and ugly in several places.

He was beginning to stir and Macey put her hands on his chest.

"Flint, can you hear me?"

He groaned and the sound tore at Macey's heart; it was that full of pain.

"It hurts," he whispered, his eyes still open but looking into the distance, not seeming to see Macey. The flames around his pupils had extinguished, but his eyes looked darker than they usually did. Like embers after they'd been quenched.

"What hurts?" Macey asked softly. Behind her,

people were running and shouting, hopefully getting a doctor.

"My magic." Suddenly, Flint moved his head and looked straight at Macey. "It's gone. He's taken it."

To be continued...

What's happening? Find out in the next book in the Seven Wardens series, Within the Flames.

And if you want to find out more about Amber and Izban's story and how they met, then take a look at Through the Storms.

Subscribe to our newsletters for all the latest books:
Skye: skyemackinnon.com/newsletter
Laura: www.authorlauragreenwood.co.uk/p/mailing-list-sign-up.html

GLOSSARY

Adlet - Inuit descendent of a dog & human

Almas - Mongolian humanoid creature

Angakok - Inuit priest/shaman

Aos Sìth - Fairy Folk

Atliarusek - Inuit gnome sized man

Baobhan Sìth - Incubus

Beithir - Venomous Reptile, a cross between a snake and a dragon

Caladrius - a snow white bird that lives in the house of a King and can heal illness and injury

Cat Sìth - Cat Shifters

Ceasg - A mermaid with a salmon tail who can grant wishes

Cù Sìth - Dog Shifters

Daimon - Guiding Spirit (Greek)

Fàth-Fiata - Magic Fog/Mist

Fedelm - Irish Celtic Prophet

Gashadokuro - Giant Japanese skeletons that bite off heads and drink blood

Kabouter - Flemish Gnomes

Kelpie - Mythical water horse

Kludde - Flemish Shapeshifter and Trickster

Lampad - Nymphs of the Underworld who bear torches. Their light can send travelers mad

Loch - Scottish word for lake

Luch - Gaelic word for mouse

Maniilaq - Inuit 19th Century prophet

Merry Dancer - Descended from fallen angels, they now make up the northern lights

Mongolian Death Worm - underground worm

Seachd-sìona - Seven Elements

Meer - Flemish for Lake

Na Fir Gorma - Storm Kelpies/Blue Men of Minch

Seelie - Light fae folk

Selkie - Man or woman who can clothe themselves in seal skin

Sìth - Faerie/Fae

Staran - Gaelic for path

Tornak - Inuit Guardian Soul

Unseelie - Dark fae folk

Watershee - A fairy like being who often acts like a siren

ABOUT LAURA GREENWOOD

Laura is a USA Today Bestselling Author of paranormal, fantasy, and urban fantasy romance (though she can occasionally be found writing contemporary romance). When she's not writing, she drinks a lot of tea, tries to resist French macarons, and works towards a diploma in Egyptology. She lives in the UK, where most of her books are set.

Follow the Author

- Website: www.authorlauragreenwood. co.uk
- Mailing List: www.authorlauragreenwood. co.uk/p/mailing-list-sign-up.html
- Facebook Group: http://facebook.com/ groups/theparanormalcouncil

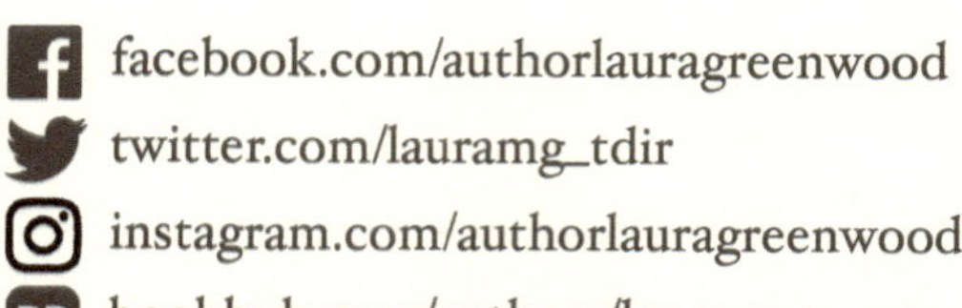

ABOUT SKYE MACKINNON

Skye MacKinnon is a USA Today & International Bestselling Author whose books are filled with strong heroines who don't have to choose.

She embraces her Scottishness with fantastical Scottish settings and a dash of mythology, no matter if she's writing about Celtic gods, cat shifters, or the streets of Edinburgh.

When she's not typing away at her favourite cafe, Skye loves dried mango, as much exotic tea as she can squeeze into her cupboards, and being covered in pet hair by her demon cat Sootie.

Subscribe to her newsletter:
skyemackinnon.com/newsletter

Join her Facebook group:
facebook.com/groups/skyesbookharem